A Christmas Reckoning

By
Arthur Wilson

© 213 Arthur Wilson
All Rights Reserved.

No part of this publication may be reproduced, stored in a retrieval system, or transmitted, in any form or by any means, electronic, mechanical, photocopying, recording, or otherwise, without the written permission of the author.

First published by Dog Ear Publishing
4010 W. 86th Street, Ste H
Indianapolis, IN 46268
www.dogearpublishing.net

dog ear
PUBLISHING

ISBN: 978-1-4575-2358-8

This book is printed on acid-free paper.

This book is a work of fiction. Places, events, and situations in this book are purely fictional and any resemblance to actual persons, living or dead, is coincidental.

Printed in the United States of America

DEDICATION

I dedicate this book to my wife Gayle, without which I would have certainly floundered in the vast sea of my adult life's challenges. She taught me by example to love and cherish being a parent and now a grandparent. I love you Gayle.

*With each life he creates
God watches and waits
For even
The smallest invitation*

*A crack in the door
Opens to so much more
For a soul
That is seeking salvation*

*You are never alone
With your sorrow
You are never alone
With your strife*

*Like the Humming Bird
With its flickering wings
He's busy loving you
All of your life*

*So open your heart
To make a fresh start
And let His angels
Do their thing*

*You can't imagine the power
They wield each minute and hour
Just to see what His love
Will bring*

ACKNOWLEDGEMENT

I want to acknowledge "Michele Metych" as the editor of my book. She suggested that this wasn't necessary because it was a work of fiction, but for me it was a major hurdle to overcome. Thank you so much, Michele.

TABLE OF CONTENTS

Dedication iii
Poem iv
Acknowledgement v

Chapter	Title	Page(s)
1	No Room?	1-20
2	Good Shepherds	21-52
3	Cut Clean	53-68
4	Signs of the Past	69-79
5	A Lifelong Challenge	80-94
6	The Secret	95-108
7	The Journey	109-126
8	A Fork in the Road	127-136
9	Gifts	137-150
10	His Answer	151-181

CHAPTER ONE

No Room?

At the end of the workday on Christmas Eve, a businessman readied himself inside a building vestibule in downtown Chicago for the nasty weather developing outside. At the same time, a heavyset fellow who was at that point oblivious to the storm, approached an adjacent set of doors. That one committed with a few steps onto the ice –covered sidewalk but then had second thoughts. After a quick turn-around he was disappointed to discover that the door he had just exited had closed and locked behind him. Seeing the other fellow come out, he yelled to him, trying to overcome the howl of the wind.

"Hold that open for a moment, would you?"

To his chagrin, it was like the man didn't hear him at all and that door locked too. The fat one, after realizing the futility that would come with vocalizing his discontent, turned quickly to look through the door glass, but there was no one else inside to come to his aid. Standing in place against the weather's onslaught was not a feasible option. All he could think to do was to head in the direction of the parking garage.

His motion, though, just served to increase the impact of the repeated blasts of freezing rain. It was like an unending attack of needle pricks on skin that was left exposed. When he tried guarding his face with an outstretched arm, the poor vision was reduced to none. In seconds he had veered off course and come within inches of slamming into a light pole. Feeling the brush of its iron against his coat sent him back on an angle toward the buildings. The ice covered walkway masked the lines and so offered no visible clue to guide him.

After struggling in this pitiable fashion against the unrelenting surges for about half a city block, he was overcome by them. In a desperate effort to find a sanctuary, he entered a narrow little covered nook that served as the entrance to an antique shop. It had already turned dark out except for the glow of the streetlights decorated for the holiday season-these though were very dim, nearly smothered by the torrent.

He was startled to see that the man who didn't hold the door had for some reason fallen behind and was now joining him there. They were both stodgy and cool in their manners from the onset, and the small space forced them to face one another. The alternative was to stand with chins almost touching the dark brick walls, and they were both much too stubborn for that. It was as if each of them thought the other was trespassing. Standing so close, they had to breathe the same air, and this served to make the situation that much more intolerable.

An alert observer of city life might have commented that this was much the same type of inconvenience experienced each day by masses of everyday people, like the ones that use buses and trains for transportation during rush hour periods. The heavy fellow however, didn't often experience that world. He was used to a much easier life. If the weather would just stop being so darned uncooperative, he could walk a short distance to the garage that housed his fine expensive vehicle. The other man by contrast had tasted the fruits of that garden but had found himself cast out.

Unlike those that cringe at parking prices but have little choice, the fat man wasn't concerned by such matters. In fact, the parking service he used catered only to those for whom the cost really didn't matter. The level of pampered service was all that really counted. It was a paid privilege that was expected by him and until this moment, not much appreciated.

Both men stared outward into the gloom. They hoped for a respite from the wild Chicago weather, but the wind seemed to only gust harder. Despite their cover, the blowing rain was soaking their pant-legs. To add to their disenchantment, water was pooling in a large dipped area that was just off the step they were standing on.

Soon the rain turned into nickel-sized chunks of ice that battered their bodies. Anyone's hope that things would soon improve would not be realized. In response to this merciless barrage, the men lifted up arms to shield their faces.

With the newly found space failing to perform as a shelter, the fat one's mind was stuck on one track. All he wanted was a reasonable way to escape into the darkness. It didn't occur to him that another scenario was unfolding.

The other man whose name is Matthew Miller did not want to escape. He was determined to stay with the fat man whose name he knew was Horace Williams. Matt was in fact irritated that Horace didn't recognize him or was ignoring him. In the end game, though, he felt that it didn't matter.

For a moment the wind changed direction. From the building side they could feel a sudden and most pleasant rush of warm air. Looking to their rear, they were surprised to see that the door to the shop had blown wide open. The hail though, returned suddenly for a second attack, and after a few seconds they both reacted as one.

Turning their bodies to face the doorway they started to advance in that direction, but found themselves as players in an old comedy routine. Their shoulders wedged together and that immediately stopped their progress. Touching? Oh no, that wouldn't do! After separating quickly, they backed to their previous stances while staring daggers at one another.

A very uncomfortable moment passed and then, Matt, who had followed finally blurted, "I'll close it, damn it! Don't bump into me!"

"Well, do it then! What are you waiting for?"

So Matt, after giving Horace a vile look, moved forward and reached in. He leaned over as if actually stepping into the place would poison him. After finally grasping the handle, he closed the door with a slam. In his move back, Matt looked at Horace as if he had bested him. He received just a grunt in response. In their heightened state of competition and their desire to separate, neither had considered the obvious sensibility of just entering the place.

The wind came at them with another blast, and the shop's door flew open yet again. Seeing this as a besting opportunity, Horace called out, "Out of the way for someone that knows how!"

With no concern for bumping into Matt he thrust his large body toward the door. To his aggravation though, he found that the door was not only open wider than before but firmly stuck in that position. He bent over and grasped the handle with two hands and put his weight into it. No matter how hard he pulled, the door just wouldn't budge. It was in fact the most physical effort his body had experienced in a long, long time. Underneath the fine overcoat and suit, his body engine was overheating, and he found himself bathed in sweat.

Recognizing his bad state, Horace overcompensated by straightening up too fast. His head grew dizzy, and his thoughts scattered. This left him unable to control his weight, and his rotund form teetered like a top that's energy was too diminished to spin upright. In a desperate reaction he leaned into the door but soon lost his balance. He then plummeted with unwillingly accelerating steps for several feet into the store.

All that saved him from going down like a KO'd prize fighter was a large wooden table stacked high with books. When he hit them, it was like the impact of a bowling ball on target with ten pins. Books flew everywhere.

The big fellow wound up in a most undignified position. The whole of him was straddling the table like a beached whale. He was left lying on top of some books that he had crushed instead of propelled. Horace had no inclination for further movement of his form, because his mind was spinning as he tried with great difficulty to regain some composure.

Finally, lucid thoughts came back, but these only served to remind him that it had already been a bad day. Early on another hurdle had confronted him. The unpleasant events of it filled his brain and he thought, "If I'm going to die soon anyway, this would be an appropriate moment!"

Horace abhorred the thought of picking himself up out of the rubble to face the other man. To him that would be a supreme slam, worse than the fall itself. He was determined to do the contrary, to carefully move from where he was laying and then without looking at his foe, he would just rush out of the place! It was of no matter to him now how bad the weather was raging or that while exiting his feet would certainly be submerged in the icy water beyond the step.

Despite all of Horace's plaguing thoughts, his lamentable condition was of no real interest to Matt except in that the fallen one was out of the race. He had already refocused.

In his insatiable quest to be a winner, he would have another go at the door. Getting behind it, he used the adjacent wall as his brace and pushed with every ounce of force he could muster. Left disgruntled after finding that it would not give, he opted to let up for just a moment to catch his breath. Yet again he tried, and this time he shook the handle violently. It just wouldn't budge! He decided to give the situation some thought while his body continued to lean into the door. In his mind he was undeterred. He would find a way whatever it took, and his thoughts revisited the motivation. His countenance could then best be described as devious.

Without warning the door gave way and caught Matt totally off guard. He tipped forward into a near fall but managed as a reflex to step outward and arrest his motion. The door by contrast was freewheeling.

The return had been bent when the door was slammed in by the wind earlier. The linkage arms wedged together and that was the reason for its sticking. Now that they had been jostled sufficiently with the shaking, nothing retarded the door's advance. It hit the jam at such a speed that the full-length pane of glass couldn't stand the shock. There was a loud crash, and the window exploded into a thousand pieces. The sizes ranged from large jagged shapes to small fragments and slivers. Many of these now formed a glistening carpet over the shop's hardwood floor in a broad area beyond the doorway.

Matt was rewarded for his determination with his own share of the glass. His dark overcoat absorbed much of it. The coat's surface reflected the shop's light with a mosaic of little glimmers. A few of the projectiles had also hit his face. It was fortunate for him that his head had been cocked away and none of the glass reached his eyes.

One nasty narrow piece however dangled from Matt's ear. Instinctively he raised his hand to the sliver, and it fell away. The wound began to ooze a deep red droplet that looked like a miniature teardrop Christmas ornament. The neck of it thinned to a thread under the weight, and he became aware of it like one would a pesky mosquito. His reactive hand motion was too late however as it suddenly plopped down to permanently mark the starched white collar of his shirt. The site of it caught the corner of his eye, and he just barely managed to stop himself from voicing his frustration.

The sounds of the door's crash and the cracking glass were quite revealing to Horace despite the fact that he was still facing down. He slowly stood up and then turned to a vision that was even worse than he had imagined. His competition had been reduced to a state of shock. Careful consideration at this point would have left Matt with little physical damage. His mind though was clouded with rage.

While focusing with horror on the busted door and floor of glass, Matt tried to back away but was stopped with a thud by the wall behind him. After looking down he noticed that his coat had a sheen like water. In his thoroughly embarrassed state, he then made the awful impulsive error of trying to brush it away with his hands.

He squealed in pain! A slew of the sharp fragments were by that sorely regretted action pressed hard into his fingers and palms. This left him frozen there, afraid to make another move as his hands throbbed with pain and a series of little red streaks appeared on them. The embarrassing fall of Horace was now dwarfed by Matt's misfortune.

Suddenly, out of the dark, a voice pierced the shop's awkward silence, "Daddy! Daddy! Are you alright? What's happening in there? Daddy!"

A quiet moment passed, and the form that matched the voice appeared in a strange portrait through what remained of the window frame. There were some odd jagged pieces still being held in it about the perimeter. The view revealed little. The hood from the form's coat and a scarf combined to cover all of the head and face except the eyes. After pulling the scarf down below the mouth, a woman's face was revealed, and she immediately demanded from Horace who was facing her, "What's going on here? Who are you and where's my father?"

Before he could respond though, she caught sight of Matt and shrieked, "What are you doing there? You can't hide from me! I see you!"

Focusing on Matt, she could see that he was covered with glass and bleeding. Her eyes moved over to the table with the books knocked all about, and she concluded quickly that the two men had been up to no good. She considered that they might have busted into the shop and attacked her father.

Cautiously backing away at first, she soon disappeared into the darkness with another shriek erupting. This was quickly followed by a frantic but faint chorus of, "Police, police, help me! Police!"

Horace tried taking a turn at remaining indifferent to the other's sorry plight. He couldn't help erupting though and sneered at him while saying, "You damned fool! Now see what you've done? She thinks we're robbing the place!"

Matt by then was feeling nauseated and responded scornfully in a low voice, "I don't give a damn what she thinks! Do you see my hands? No, I take that back, I hope that she does think we are robbers. Not to say that there is one thing in here worth taking. If someone comes back, I might at least get some help. More than I could expect from you, you miserable old bastard!"

Horace was taken back by this angry verbal escalation and remained silent for a moment. After which he retorted with, "Well, you should expect no more than you gave me when I fell. As for old, you clumsy ass, I would wager that you are older than I am!"

Matt shot back with, "You're deluding yourself. By the looks of you, your heart could fail at any second. That is if you even have one! I saw the way you stumbled backward after pulling on that door for a moment! Death is on your doorstep. The grim reaper will grow grimmer still when he sees that he has to retrieve the likes of you!"

Horace had quickly decided that the other was determined to continue on with his rant and so was only partially listening to the onslaught. He could be quite impervious when he had a mind to be. It was a skill he learned from his father when warding off his mother's onslaughts. Instead he tried to call out on his cell phone, but found that it wouldn't operate. With frustration he exclaimed, "Damned fool things, never work when you really need them!"

This time before Matt could respond critically again, another voice could be heard from beyond the entrance, "Julie, Julie are you in there?"

Horace responded loudly, "There's no Julie in here! Call for some help, would you? There's a man hurt! He's cut and bleeding. The glass door busted and showered him with glass!"

Caught off guard by this appearance of consideration, Matt stared over at him puzzled. Horace though, when seeing this reaction, quickly exclaimed, "I'm not doing this for you! It's true that some authority like the police are what's needed now to resolve this situation! I won't be called a thief!"

The wind howled and a man's voice rang out again, "A thief, no, I'm not a thief!"

The form of a man appeared, in the manner of his predecessor. Matt could see that he was holding something high against his chest. It was wrapped in a blanket.

The man outside spoke up with emphasis, "I have to get my baby in from the weather! It's treacherous out here!"

He held the infant snug to his jacket and stepped through the door's hole with a crunch onto the scattered glass. While passing the fat man he exclaimed to him, "Wow, it's like a war zone in here! What did you do, break in to get out of the storm?"

Without waiting for an answer, he pushed away some remaining books from a spot on the table and placed his blanketed bundle down. He parted the folds and then smiled and sighed when he saw the light blue eyes of a sweet chubby-faced baby stare back at him.

This prompted him to look up and exclaim, "Whew! I was worried that the little guy couldn't breathe right with the way I had wrapped him up! It's so awful out there with the rain and sleet and hail. And that darned wind; it blew us right across the street! Fortunately, no one's driving out there now, and you would have to be nuts to try! It's a terrible storm. You can't see your hand in front of your face!"

Matt spoke up, "Did you run into anyone out there anywhere that could help me?"

"No, why?

After which he looked over at Matt and seeing that he was bleeding, called out, "Hey, man! You're in a bad way! What the heck happened here?"

"The door exploded on me! I was trying to close it, but it was stuck. It suddenly came loose, and the impact with the frame made it shatter! If I could get the glass out of my hands, I could help myself!"

The man with the baby looked around the room and replied, "Sure, I'll help you! Just stay still!"

He looked back over at Horace and instructed, "Hey, you there! Make sure my baby doesn't roll off the table! Can you do that?"

"Why, certainly I can! Do you think I'm an imbecile?"

"Well, I don't know what you are! You've been standing over there just watching while your pal here is bleeding!"

"He's no acquaintance of mine, and besides, it just happened. The fool brought it on himself by rubbing his hands on his glass covered coat!"

The younger man stared back at him with contempt and stated, "Does it really matter how or why it happened? He's bleeding and needs help!"

With that said he proceeded to pan the room. He turned and walked behind a desk in the rear of the shop and pulled out an old chair. After dragging it across the room, he set it in a spot where the floor was clear of glass. While walking over to Matt, that one started to move toward him. Seeing this, he exclaimed, "Just a second there now! Stand still! I'll unfasten your coat."

Matt did as he asked, and the one offering the aid added, "Let your arms hang straight down! When the coat is unbuttoned, I'm going to work my hands in carefully and get the coat up over your shoulders. After I do that, just let it drop to the floor, ok?"

Matt shook his head to the affirmative. The process as described began. As the younger man's hands slipped carefully under the coat and started moving up Matt's chest, the room went totally black! This was followed by a voice crying out, "No, stop, oh!"

And another screamed, "Ow, son of a bitch! What are you doing?"

With that, there were some additional noises of the men stumbling about and the crunching of glass. After a little time lapsed the light came back on.

Horace standing by the baby could see Matt standing there, uttering, with his coat still in place, "I didn't mean to do that, but the lights went out and I thought!"

He stopped short of finishing. The younger man stood hunched over holding his arm and replied angrily, "You thought what? What the hell made you grab my wrist? Now there are two of us wounded here! Why didn't you just hold still? Son of a bitch, that hurts!"

"I felt your hand uh, by...by my billfold, and the light went out. I...I didn't know what to think!"

The younger man looked at him astonished and fought to form his words. After an uncomfortable moment he sputtered out, "You ass! I trusted my baby to a total stranger so I could come to your aid, and you thought I was robbing you! How cynical can you get?"

"I'm sorry, you are right. I'm so sorry, I made a mistake!"

"You're damned right you did! I have half a mind to let you just stand there and bleed! Look at my wrist!"

In a couple of minutes, the younger man regained his normal civil demeanor, and he stated to the one bleeding, "Look mister if you promise not to do anything else stupid, I'll help you get that coat off, and move you over to that chair. You obviously need to get off your feet!"

Matt agreed, and the younger one proceeded with the coat removal successfully this time. He then swung Matt's arm over his shoulder to support him. As they moved, Matt stated again, "I'm sorry, I'm really sorry!"

The wounded man was let down in the chair by the younger one as easily as possible considering that he was just using his good hand. Matt just slumped down. He wished that he could bury his face in his hands but that bit of solace was denied him. The younger man told him then to lean back the best he could. Matt did so and rested his head against the nearby counter's edge.

Satisfied with Matt's more stable position, the younger man walked back to the desk and retrieved an ornate looking ashtray with a dragon body shape. He placed it on the counter next to Matt and called to Horace, "Listen here now we need something to use as an antiseptic and some bandages. Some tweezers too, would be a godsend! There appears to be a lot of different stuff in here. Go look and see if you can find something that might be useful. Meanwhile I'm going to pick some of this glass out of my wrist."

As Horace turned to act on that, the younger one added, "Wait just a second. What's your name, in case I have to call you again?"

"Horace, my name is Horace."

"And what's his name?"

"I told you. I don't know him! We both came to this place at the same time by chance."

"Well ok then, go and do what I asked. We've got to work together here. Who knows how long we'll be trapped in this place. Damn, I hope this storm ends soon and my Julie's alright. I've got to find her! Do you understand? My wife, this little guy's mother, is out there in that nasty storm somewhere. I've got to find her! I wish that we never came to the city!"

Horace thought for a second about what the fellow had said and replied, "Just a minute or so before you arrived here there was a young woman that came near the door. She was calling for her daddy. When she saw us, and with this one bleeding, she thought we were robbing the place. She backed out yelling for the police and then disappeared."

The young man got excited hearing this and quickly approached Horace, grabbed his coat lapel and demanded, "A woman, you say a woman was here? What did she look like?"

Horace described her dress the best that he could remember. To this the young man exclaimed, "God help her! That sounds like it could be my Julie! You said though, that she was calling for her daddy? That doesn't sound right!"

He considered that a moment and added to himself, "She did ask me to come with her downtown for a surprise, but her daddy, I can't figure that!"

In a second he asked Horace, "Where is the owner of this place?"

"There was no one here when the wind blew the door open, at least not in this room! We never went into the back."

"Well, let's check it out!"

He sped over to a wood rear door. Horace followed. The young fellow, after grasping the door handle, found that it wouldn't turn and stated in an exasperated tone, "It appears to be locked!"

Horace also gave it a try using both his hands with no success. After his earlier folly he gave up readily and added, "Yes, tight as a drum!"

As Horace looked around further, something caught his eye and he stated, "Look there!"

Back behind the desk that he guessed was used by the proprietor or a hired clerk, there was a wooden box hanging on the wall. It looked about the size of a medicine cabinet and had a red cross on it.

This discovery gave them some hope that it held the medical supplies that were needed. Horace opened it and found that it was filled with little bottles that appeared to have been used for medical purposes. The problem that soon became obvious though was that they appeared to be very old. Further inspection revealed that they were also empty. Horace dismissed them as being antiques like the rest of the shop's holdings.

Disappointed, but not deterred by this, the younger man approached the desk and opened a drawer. Finding nothing of use in that one, he opened the one under it, and after shuffling some things about he smiled broadly while calling out, "All right now, here's something!"

He held up a little plastic container of generic painkiller tablets and stated with enthusiasm, "These should definitely help our cause!"

After that he spun around and grabbed a coffee cup from the desktop and handed it to Horace while saying, "Here, wipe this out with something, and get us some water!"

"Get some water, where?"

"Just look outside and use your imagination!"

Horace looked at the fellow's smile that followed and uttered in response an annoyed, "Harrumph!"

After giving the situation some thought, Horace pushed the front of his overcoat aside and dug deep down into his pants pocket. He removed a white monogrammed handkerchief and was about to use it to clean the cup. This caught the younger man's attention, and he interrupted Horace with, "Hold on there!"

While approaching him, he added, "Is that clean? Have you used it?"

"Why, of course it's clean! No, I haven't blown my nose in it if that's what you are asking!"

"Well, that's good then, give it to me! Use something else to wipe out the cup. This is the closest thing to a bandage that we have right now!"

While looking at the cup, Horace considered what was said and added in a matter-of-fact tone, "Any self-respecting gentleman would have a clean handkerchief! In fact, I believe I have another one inside my coat!"

The younger man, after assessing that he had none, gave Horace a wry look and replied, "Well, ok, that's great! Now we're getting somewhere. Do you suppose the fellow bleeding over there might have a couple of those tucked away too?"

"It wouldn't surprise me!"

He thought about how his answer implied that his bleeding foe of the night was a gentleman. He stopped himself short of adding something harsh to counter it. With Horace's reaction understood, the younger fellow smiled and then walked over to the bleeding man who had his eyes closed. He nudged him gently and asked, "Hey there fella, what's your name?"

Matt opened his eyes and focused. He responded in a lethargic manner with, "My name? Oh, yes, I forgot for a moment where I was. My name is Matt... Matthew Miller!"

Horace, when hearing this, took notice. The name sounded familiar and he tried to place it. The younger man then added, "Ok, Matt, my name is Stash and your partner in crime over there is Horace! We're trying to pull ourselves together to deal with this bleeding situation. We've located some pain pills, and we'll give you some in a moment. What we need more of is something to make bandages with. Do you have a clean handkerchief?"

"Yes, I do! I have one in my pants pocket, and I believe there's also one in my overcoat."

Horace smiled at Stash with an air of satisfaction. Stash questioned Matt further with, "Well, are they clean?"

"Well, they should be! You have to be careful though, not to get glass on the one in my overcoat. It's in the left hand pocket."

After realizing that unintentionally he had been ribbed by the two men in the last minute for not having a handkerchief, Stash responded a little satirically, "Yah right, I'll be careful!"

In a few minutes, Horace returned with some snow in the cup and stated, "It's turned into a real blizzard out there. The temperature has dropped and I couldn't see a single person or vehicle on the street! When this snow in here melts though, there'll be some water."

Stash replied while shivering, "I don't know if it'll melt at all, as cold as it's starting to get in here!"

There was the sound of the wind whining behind them in the entrance, and this prompted him to add, "We need to block that door with something!"

Horace replied, "Yes, but with what?"

Matt lifted one of his bleeding hands and pointed across the room. On the far wall behind a couple of shelves and some tall pieces of old furniture were a couple of posters. One showed two characters from an old western TV series. It was a cigarette endorsement. Beside it was another with a large red-faced Santa Claus holding a bottle of Coke.

Stash, after seeing these exclaimed, "Matt, I think you're onto something there!"

He looked to Horace and instructed, "Get those poster boards, would you, and use them to block the door opening. We'll all feel better if it warms up in here!"

"And use what to hold them up there?"

Stash gave him another look, but before he could reply, Horace added, "I know, I know, use my imagination!"

Stash smiled and responded with, "There you go, Horace! Now you're learning!"

As Horace made his way to the other side of the shop, he got a good look at the poster boards. It then also became clear that there was a large and long floor-standing counter that was blocking his access to them.

A close inspection of the enclosure revealed that it was made mostly of glass. He looked down into it while considering getting the chair that Matt was sitting on to help him to reach the poster boards. The case's interior caught his interest though. He focused on the remnants of someone's old collection of little pewter soldiers. He remembered having such a set when he was a boy. It was one of only a few fun things that his mother had ever indulged him with. He thought, "Oh, the hours I played with those figures!"

The detailed little Civil War set of his youth had been precious to him. It was complete with soldiers representing both the blue and grey in various positions of marching and fighting. Some were standing, others were kneeling while shooting rifles, and others were mounted on horses. There were also tents, campfires, artillery, wagons, and flags.

He would create elaborate scenes with these on hills, by rivers, bridges, and around towns. No sooner would he complete one, that he would take it down and start another. The set was probably the main resource that he utilized at the time to stir his imagination.

"In fact," he considered, "they were likely the reason for much of the success in business that I garnered afterward."

The playing had led to his reading countless books on the Civil War. He could talk once of all the strategies that had been documented about key battle successes as well as the reasons for those that had failed. Later on as an adult he would use this information to fight the battles of the competitive business world. He would pool his resources, plan his attacks and outflank those that tried to oppose him. His success had been notable. In his field he had climbed to claim a spot near the top of the heap.

As his mind rampaged about in those old memories he was suddenly brought back to reality by a shout from Stash, "Hey there, are you getting those boards or what?"

"I need something to climb on! Oh, never mind, I found it!"

On the floor to his right he spotted an old red leather ottoman. He considered, "I used to have one of these too! I wonder what happened to it?"

He tried lifting the piece, but it was too wide and heavy for him to manage. Instead, he did his best to nudge it along the wood floor with his knee while using the counter as a steady rest. As he did this, he noticed something else in the glass counter and exclaimed, "Ahah!"

In a few moments Horace came to the other side of the shop toting the two poster boards. Stash spotted him and said, "That's good, Horace! If you can block off that cold blast, it'll be great."

By this point Stash was leaning back against the table while working to remove a piece of glass from Matt's hand with his fingers. It was tedious and difficult work. He was getting frustrated with how the day had brought him to this point. His stomach was churning with worry about his wife, who was somewhere out in the storm.

That's when Horace interrupted his thought while wearing a satisfied grin with, "I found something that I think will lift your spirits a bit!"

He opened a small old leather case. It was a man's grooming set filled with little tools like nail clippers and a cuticle cleaner. The best find though was not one but two different-sized tweezers. Stash spotted these and exclaimed, "Oh, thank God! Give me one of those!"

Grasping the tweezers, he set about quickly removing some pieces of glass that were still stuck in his own wrist. This turn of events pumped him up with a new enthusiasm. He completed his own little surgeries and returned to work methodically on the glass in Matt's hand.

Suddenly he stopped and stated in a serious tone, "Look, Horace, you need to help Matt now! Work on this hand that I started here first and get it wrapped up with a handkerchief. One probably won't be enough so you might have to use what's left after I do mine. If you need more, rip some strips from your shirt. It looks clean enough!"

Horace's eyes widened at this, but Stash continued undeterred with, "Once I finish getting myself wrapped up here, I have to go out and look for my wife! I can't take the baby, though. It's too damned nasty out there. You're going to have to watch him for me!"

At this Horace took on a look of disbelief and exclaimed in defiance, "Now look here! It is one thing for me to nursemaid this fellow, but I know nothing about caring for a baby! I never have. That's impossible!"

Stash stared at him then with a look of desperation and pleaded, "Look, Horace. I can see that this is a tough thing for you, but you've just got to help me! My little guy is a good baby. He hardly ever cries. If he does, it's just for one of two things. He's either hungry or needs to be changed! There's a milk bottle and some diapers in this bag over here. There's nothing to it! Would you help me, please? I've just got to find my wife. If something happens to her, I don't know what I would do!"

Something in Stash's words hit deep down at a tender spot in Horace's past. He went into a zone for a minute, but was suddenly shaken out of it by Stash's cry! "Horace, don't blank out on me now!"

Horace focused on him and Stash repeated, "Horace, will you help me? I really need you!"

To this Horace finally answered in a low tone, "I'll do what I can."

"Thanks, man! You'll do just fine. You can be sure that one way or another I'll get back here in a while to get little Johnny."

As he struggled to bandage his own wrist, Stash blurted out with frustration, "Can you help me wrap this? In that baby bag there should be a clean bib. You can wrap that around the handkerchiefs I used and then tie it. That will have to do until I can get some antiseptic. If I locate some, I'll bring it back with me so we can help Matt better! Maybe we'll be lucky, and I will find a cop. I sure hope so!"

In a moment he added with frustration, "I'm not sure where to look for my wife. The last place we were at together was the train station. I haven't been in Chicago since I was a little boy and don't know my way around! Julie gave me directions earlier to get to this place and meet her, but I found myself getting lost. I kept going round and round the blocks. These big buildings all look the same to me!"

He paused while thinking and added, "She said that she had to get something that was part of a surprise. I thought after getting lost, that she might have beaten me here. Maybe she did, if that was Julie you told me about. When I finally saw the right street sign I was so relieved, but I went the wrong way I guess. The numbers are so damn confusing. I couldn't find the shop; there was no number like the one that she showed me. So I turned back, and this wicked storm blew up. I couldn't believe it when I ducked into this place, and it had the right address. I just couldn't believe it!"

Horace explained, "I think I know what happened to you. You see, the numbers all start with zero at the intersection of State and Madison. You have to know whether the address you're seeking is north, south, east, or west and go in that direction until a building number matches the one you're looking for. It's not hard to understand how a stranger can get lost. Now and again I still lose track if I go to an unfamiliar area, and I've been coming downtown for over forty years!"

By that point Stash's mind had started to drift somewhere else. He absorbed only a part of what Horace had said and then thought aloud, "I wonder if she went back to the station. I wish my cell phone worked in here!"

Horace added something about getting to the station, but he wasn't sure if Stash had taken it in.

Stash blurted out, "That's what I need to do first. When I get outside, I'll try to call the police."

After a short period he added, "I wish Julie had taken the cell phone. She insisted that I have it, because I have the baby."

Horace watched intently as Stash pushed up the collar of his plaid coat and then pulled a red sock hat down over his ears. He set about carefully walking through the broken door while avoiding the remaining jagged glass pieces. Once past it he turned his head momentarily and called back, "Get this covered now, Horace! I'll see you in a while, hopefully with my wife!"

With that he disappeared into the darkness from whence he had come.

CHAPTER TWO

Good Shepherds

*I*n a white brick tri-level house located on a typically small city lot near Midway Airport, a grey-haired, flush-faced man of somewhat advanced age was sitting at his kitchen table. He was eating supper with his wife and pleased with both the aroma and taste of this day's selection of beef stew. It had been slow cooking in a crock pot for several hours.

As he mopped up the remainder of some brown gravy with a piece of buttered bread, he commented, "It's turnin' into quite a night out there, with the blowin' wind and sleet! It'll be a great one to just sit and snuggle by the fireplace."

Beyond them was a cozy little living room with a fire in the hearth and a lot of little decorations for the holiday. In front of a bay window was a short and stubby balsam decked out with all the trimmings. It was lit by the older style large bulbs of red, orange, green, yellow, blue, and white rather than the miniatures that were far more common. The tree had a rich aroma, and it twinkled randomly while the lights reflected on glass ornaments and tinsel in motion as heated air streamed up from a register in the floor. On top of the tree was a star that would have seemed quite commonplace except for a ring of angels that was just below it.

He gave his wife, Kate, a wink and added, "You know it's the first Christmas Eve I've had off in five years!"

"Yes, and I'm high tempted to pull the plug on the phone!"

"I know, my love. I've had the same temptation myself, but it's not my way."

"Yes, it's true, like father like son!"

"And what is the matter with that?"

"Well, it's my opinion that your poor mother didn't have much of a life, with your dad on the street all the time. I'm thankful to see you a little more than she saw him!"

"Yes, we have a better life, don't we?"

Before she could answer, he added, "We do and yet we don't. It's a kind of paradox!"

"What do you mean? Are you getting philosophical with me now? That's not a side of you I've seen much of in our thirty-five years together!"

"I must not be, my dear, cause I can't even pronounce it!"

To this she laughed.

In a few seconds, he added, "I've been tryin' to put my finger on it and all I can figure is that in some ways life is actually harder now!"

"Ok, Mike, where are you goin' with this? Just spit it out! I can tell somethin' is smokin' in your broiler!"

After gathering his thoughts the best he could, he replied, "Well, it's true that dad's generation had a lot of hell to deal with while living through the Depression, World War II, and Korea. They also certainly had a lot less in terms of material things. I mean, both of our folks had to live with their parents or other relatives when they were married, and your dad had one hell of a hard job in the stockyards!"

He caught his breath and continued with, "The fact is though, that people were satisfied with less back then. Now, they gotta have everything they see, like big screen TVs, fancy cars, video games, and cell phones that change by the day. The expectations are so high that it's making life harder for everyone. For a lot of folks nuthin's good enough, and some want everything without workin' for it.

"To make things worse, even if they do work for it, stuff is gettin' out of reach. Take our Angie for example. How will she and Fred ever afford a home? A guy from work told me that places in Bridgeport are goin' for over three hundred thousand dollars, and some for half a million and more—even with the economy being so bad! Can you believe it? When my mom sold our two-flat there just ten years ago she got forty seven thousand dollars, and that place was a little jewel. I wish now that she had hung onto it. Angie and Fred didn't want to live in the city then. Bet they'd have a different opinion now!"

Kate spoke up with, "Well, maybe now the kids will come to their senses and save some money. It's true that things cost more, but they make more money than we did at their age. If they want a house they'll just have to get their priorities straight. They might have to move out away from the city to find a place."

"Yes, but how far? I heard that prices are ridiculous all the way out in Mokena in the far southwest. Do you remember goin' to my cousin Ryan's wedding out there? My God, that's just a farm town. It takes an hour to drive out there! Where will the kids have to move to afford a place—Rock Island?"

"Honey, I worry about that too, but they'll work it out somehow. When we spent sixty five thousand for this place, your mother thought we were crazy. She was thinkin' in terms of her time, and you're thinkin' in terms of ours. Angie and Fred both have decent jobs and that's somethin' to be real thankful for.

"Yah, but what if a baby or two come along? What will they do then?"

After considering this for a moment, Kate answered, "Well, if they're smart, they'll pray for God's help, just like we did!"

"No problem too big for Him, huh?"

"Not as far as I'm concerned!"

Mike put his arm around her waist and while pulling her over to him, said, "Come on over here, my little Christmas present. You were the answer to my prayers!"

She sat on his lap and gave him a big kiss on his cheek, leaving an imprint of red lipstick. Just then the phone rang, and Kate jumped up and exclaimed, "Oh shit!"

Realizing what she had said, she quickly begged the Lord's pardon and made the sign of the cross! Mike shot up himself and with a finger held in front of his mouth, signaled for Kate to be quiet. After which he went to answer the phone.

In a minute he came back and said to her in a low voice, "I'm sorry, my love, but they've called me in."

Her face grew sad, and she answered disappointedly, "Oh, Mike, can't we get just one Christmas?"

"It's the darn storm, they tell me. Two main electrical stations have gone down, and power's out in half of downtown. They're expecting the storm to turn into a raging blizzard. Could be another "67! There's already been a record high of accidents on the roads and all hell is breakin' loose. They're callin' in everyone!"

Kate just sighed and stated in a dejected tone, "Well your uniform's hanging on the door. Make sure you take your heavy coat! And don't be volunteerin' for tomorrow for God sakes, let the younger ones pull their weight!"

"Yes, my love! I'll be back before you can say, 'Jimmy Crack Corn!'

She immediately started to say it, but he put a hand to her mouth and added with a smile, "Now you have to give me a chance to leave, before sayin' it! You know the rules."

To that she didn't respond. She just watched as he changed into his uniform and assisted him the best she could as she had so many times before in his long career as a Chicago police officer.

Finally, as Mike was at the door ready to leave, she kissed him again on the cheek and said mischievously, "Now if you come home before I get to sleep, I might just let you unwrap one Christmas present a little early!"

He replied with a grin, "Hmmmm, I'll keep that in mind!"

A second later he grabbed hold of the door handle and added, "Seriously my love, I wish and pray that I could have just one Christmas Eve that something nice happens so that I can keep in the spirit of things. I've had my fill this week of the drug addicts, prostitutes, break-ins, shootings, night club fights, crazy teenagers runnin' amuck, and heart breakin' car accidents! I guess I'm getting too damned old for this job."

With that said she gave him a serious look as he put on his hat and gloves and then raised his collar. He walked out slowly onto the concrete stoop and then off into the night to make ready his snow-covered sedan for a predictably tense drive in the storm.

* * *

On the west side of the city, in an old three-level brick apartment building facing a park, a Hispanic family was in the throes of finishing their meal. There was a serious problem that needed resolution, and the adults stayed by the kitchen table talking. If it had been a financial issue they would have taken it in stride. That would have been considered normal. Everyone that was able was expected to work and so far when they pool their resources, there was enough to keep a roof over their heads and just enough food in their bellies.

They were a resourceful group and managed to fit nine in a flat with three small bedrooms. You might say that they had four if you counted the porch outside the kitchen. The oldest male, Jesse, had managed to enclose and heat it with an electric space heater. If you counted the porch though, you should then also count the dining room with the sofa that converts into a double bed at night.

This group, who went by the last name Sanchez, were actually three families in one. The first of these was made up of Jesse's grandparents that had volunteered from the first days there to sleep in the dining room, because they stayed up late and were early risers. It was a dining room by name only. Filling the room was the foldout bed, an old china cabinet that held their everyday dishes, and the stove that heated the flat.

Then there was Jesse's mom and his siblings. That included two sisters, Theresa and Santia, and a brother, Ernie. Finally, there was Jesse with his wife, Maria, and their daughter, who was named after his mother, Delores. Jesse and his wife had the first bedroom. Delores and little Delores shared the second, and the two sisters had the third. Jesse's younger brother Ernie slept on the porch.

This arrangement seemed to work out fine for Ernie in all but the coldest days of winter when he would come in and sleep on the other couch in the living room. The potential problem with his doing this was that the living room was where the grandparents sat late at night watching TV. Sometimes others would watch too. It was their main means of learning the English language. It was common for them to mimic words and sentences out loud that they had just heard.

If Ernie slept on the couch, everyone had to go to sleep or possibly sit in the kitchen. Often though, Jesse's sisters would be doing homework at the kitchen table. Their bedroom was small, like all the others. It only fit a bunk bed and a small dresser with just a little walking space left over.

There was just one bathroom in the flat, but it held the newest fixtures. The landlord had replaced the tub, toilet, and sink just before the Sanchezes moved in. They were thrilled that it also had a shower. It turned out to be the most desirable room in the flat, and its use had to be managed continuously.

The apartment only had two small closets, so things like bulky winter coats, and boots, were kept on a rack in the living room. Things that could be stored away that wouldn't fit in the closets were kept in stacked boxes on the porch behind Ernie's bed.

It would be obvious to anyone taking all of this in, that with so many folks living in close proximity to one another, a great deal of cooperation was required. And so, everyone was pretty aware of each other's daily routines. If a problem was developing, it was hard to keep it a secret.

The problem being discussed this evening focused on Ernie. He had started high school in the fall and was dealing with a lot of adjustments. One of these had recently become very serious. Jesse was informed of the nature of Ernie's problem that night just before leaving for work. He was the oldest male having experience with schools in the U.S. and as such was expected to resolve it.

He found Ernie's situation to be a tough challenge and was upset that it came just on time for Christmas. Until that juncture, the holiday had held a lot of promise of better times, not for just Ernie, but all of them. Now a crack was created in their foundation and its effect was spreading fast into the fragile framework of the family's existence.

Jesse knew that this was a challenge that couldn't be put off. He put on his coat and walked back through the flat and onto the porch. He faced Ernie, who was sitting on his bed with his head hanging down and his eyes staring blankly at the red, gold, and black patterns on a throw rug.

Jesse broke the silence with, "It's too cold out here to sleep Ernie! How about coming inside? I need to talk with you!"

Ernie didn't respond, in fact, he failed to even look up.

Jesse added, "Hey, man, look at me! I want to talk with you, and I don't have much time before I leave for work!"

Ernie still looked down but finally answered in a low voice with, "Go ahead and leave! I'm not making you stay."

Jesse responded while sitting down on the bed next to him, "I hear that you've got a problem at school! How about telling me about it?"

"There's nuthin' you can do! I'm goin' to take care of this by myself!"

"That's the problem. The way you're gonna take care of it!"

Jesse looked around the room and queried, "Where is it, Ernie? Where's the gun?"

Ernie again didn't respond. So Jesse got up and started to shuffle through the drawers of Ernie's dresser. Finding nothing, he turned and instructed him, "Get up! Get off of the bed!"

Ernie didn't react, and Jesse grabbed his arm and pulled him up. He then lifted the mattress and found the object of the search, a little Saturday Night Special!

Ernie yelled, "Leave it be! It's mine!"

Jesse reached down and picked up the gun while giving it a once-over. He had enough personal experience with the subject to state, "Listen, dumb shit! The only thing this is goin' to get you is dead!"

"I'll be dead one way or another. They're gonna kill me! Don't you understand? I have no choice! When I return to school after the holiday, they'll be waitin' for me!"

Jesse got a solemn look on his face, and after a moment he asked, "Who will be waiting?"

"The Desperadoes!" Either I join or get wasted! Either way I lose. The initiation is to shoot one of their enemies! If I do that, the other gang will be after me, or I'll go to jail, or both. There's no way out! Don't you see? There's no way out!"

Jesse thought for a second and then sat down on the bed and put his arms around Ernie. While hugging him he replied, "I'll help you, bro! There's an answer to this! I'll help you find it!"

Ernie exclaimed while pushing back hard against him, "What's the answer? You tell me just one way that I can beat this!"

After a moment of thinking, Jesse replied, "The first thing is, if you don't go back to school, then they won't get to you, right?"

"You're sayin' for me to drop out of school? Then what? You're contradicting yourself, man! You told me before that I'll have no future without school!"

"I'm not saying to drop out! What we'll do is transfer you to another school!"

Ernie shot back, "I heard that it's the same with any of the schools near here. If its not one gang, its another! Besides, they wouldn't let me transfer anyway!"

Jesse felt relieved then that his brother was actually thinking of the alternatives and replied, "It's not that way with the Catholic schools!"

"Catholic schools, now you're sounding like momma! Where are we goin' to get the money for a Catholic school? We hardly got enough to eat!"

"Look, man, I'm workin' on a deal to get my own business. If that happens, I can use money I make from it to help you with school, and you can work with me there too!"

Ernie just stared back at him for a second wearing a look of disbelief and responded, "You're just makin' that shit up! How are you going to get a business?"

"Look, bro, momma said that she'll help me with some money that was going to be mine for college. I convinced her that what I need it for is a business. If the idea doesn't pan out, we'll use the money just for a private school for you. Everyone agreed on it! Either way, you're not going back to the one this gang is at! Do you understand? We won't let that happen!"

Ernie sat back down on the bed and started to sob while saying, "You'll do that for me?"

"Of course we will, man! We're family! We Sanchezes stick together!"

* * *

Back in the high-rise building that housed the antique shop, on its first floor, a young black man was taking a work break and talking to his wife on the company phone. It was near the start of the conversation that he asked sincerely, "Baby, what's the matter? You're sounding down!"

His wife, Gala, replied, "They laid me off from the Jeffrey Company!"

This set him back for a moment, and he replied sadly, "Oh, no!"

He caught himself quickly though and took a more upbeat tone with, "Well don't worry, baby, we talked about this. You'll get whatever job you can for a little while and then something better will eventually turn up. You're really smart and can do a lot of stuff that I don't even understand. We'll get through this!"

"I know, Charles, but why did this have to happen right before Christmas? It puts a dark cloud over the whole holiday."

"Look, babe, there's no sense getting all blue. There's nothing we can do about it. You didn't like your boss there anyway. He was always acting weird! I'm glad now that you're not going back. That guy gave me the creeps when I met him briefly the day that I picked you up. I think he's on something."

After thinking a second he added, "Besides, you told me that their whole business is just hanging on by a thread anyway!"

"Yes, I guess you're right! I suppose it is for the best. At least I'll be home with Elsie for a while when I'm not job searching, and you'll see more of her too each day before you go to work. She'll love that! There's no sense bringing her to day care. We can't afford it now anyway."

"That's good, babe, think on the bright side! It shows that there's at least one good thing that will happen now with my being on this evening shift! Everything will be cool, I promise!"

"The thing I'm not looking forward to is being stuck here at home with your grandfather, Charles. The man drives me crazy!"

"I know he's been acting a little strange this last year but that's because he's lonely!"

"Lonely, lonely for what? You're his grandson!"

"Babe, he's lonely for the other men he used to hang out with in our old neighborhood. After my mom died he was lost. She did everything for him. That's when he started hanging out with those guys. They were his main ties to the past."

"Those old farts that sit by the liquor store? No one in their right mind would be missing them. They just gossip and drink and drink and gossip!"

Charles broke into her rant with, "They also play cards and checkers. They're all older than heck! What do you expect them to do?"

"Well, for one thing they could all use a good soaking and scrubbing with some powerful soap. They stink to the high heavens!"

"Gala, you're exaggerating!"

She backed off a little with her tone then while saying, "Well, not by much."

Charles waited a second to add, "I know you're feeling bad about losing your job, but don't take it out on my grandfather. We're all he has now. He's trying to adjust! You've seen how he loves our yard, and last week I found a nature magazine on the table in his room. I think he's planning a garden! Wouldn't that be nice? It would give him something to do."

After absorbing this for a moment, Gala replied, "A garden would be nice if he would keep it up! It would also be something he could do with Elsie sometimes. She would like to go by him, but he shuts himself up in his room most of the time.

While we're on the subject of your grandfather, you said that you would talk with him. I want to have the couple next door over for a visit. If he refers to Thomas as 'Uncle Tom' one more time, I think they will decide not to have anything to do with us!"

"You're really unloading on me tonight, babe! Are you almost out of bullets?"

Gala laughed and added, "Well, just one more. How is Elsie doing over there? I was really shocked when I read your note that you had taken her in with you! Charles, are you sure you won't get in trouble? That's all we need now, for both of us to lose our jobs! The bottom would fall out! We would lose our home!"

Charles considered the reality of that statement but forced himself to continue to be upbeat by saying, "Don't worry babe, I've got it all under control. She's tucked away where only I can get to her. You know that I promised her! What else could I do?"

"Well, if you're sure, but have you looked at the weather? It's getting awful outside here—how is it downtown?"

"I really haven't had a chance to look out, but I know the power went out once, because I had to turn our generator on. I hurried and."

Gala broke in excitedly, "Oh, Charles, when the power was out, what happened to Elsie?"

"Gala, it's alright! She's fine! It was only for about a half minute, and after I turned the generator back on, I checked on her. She just asked what happened and when I told her, she said, 'I'm ok!' and she was!"

"She must have been terrified being in the dark!"

"It didn't stay dark where she is. There are battery-powered lights that go on automatically. When I got the generator back on, the regular lights worked, and her little TV turned back on too! She's Ok! You know I wouldn't lie to you!"

"Alright, I believe you, but I'm asking you now, if the weather keeps up like this, don't stop to see that manger scene! I know that you promised her, but her safety and health have to come first!"

"I know, babe! I understand."

It was Charles' turn to have an afterthought. He asked, "Honey, did you find out if your mom is coming for Christmas?"

There was a period of silence, after which Gala replied in an unconvincing tone, "I haven't heard from her."

"You mean you haven't called her yet!"

"I called her the last time. It's her turn!"

"Babe, don't be stubborn about this now. If your mother doesn't come over for Christmas, Elsie will be heartbroken! If you don't call her, I will!"

"Charles, don't you dare!"

"Babe, I'm getting real tired of these battles of will between you and your mother. What are you arguing about now?"

"I wasn't arguing. I just told her that it would be nice if she would start going out. She's not that old, and it's silly for her to be all alone!"

Charles thought that it was ironic that she was concerned about her mom's having company but couldn't understand why his grandfather was so lonely. He knew better than to bring it up though. This conversation was already strung out too long. Instead he commented, "I'm sure she'll start going out when she meets the right man."

"That's just what she told me! Charles, have you been talking to my mother behind my back?"

Charles reacted to this, thinking, "Shit, I can't say anything right!"

Finally he replied, "No, babe I didn't talk to your mother!"

There was a small silent moment before he added, "I've got to get back to work now. We'll talk more about your job and everything tomorrow. We'll have a nice Christmas, you'll see. I love you, babe!"

Sensing his irritation, she let it end and replied, "I love you too, honey. Please be real careful comin' home with Elsie, bye!"

Charles was glad that he was able to get Gala off the subject of her job. He only wished that he felt confident about what he had told her. They were just managing to make ends meet with both of their checks. He thought, "Man, I hope she's able to get another job soon!"

He rolled over in his mind how committed they were with a large mortgage payment. Just the year before they had bought a little house in a south suburb called Richton Park. Gala loved the place and would be devastated if they had to give it up. It has a nice big yard and a swing set for Elsie, their little four-year-old. They also have friendly neighbors with little kids too. Several of them were around Elsie's age.

A couple of the families that they met there shared the experience of having fled from their inner city neighborhoods that were plagued with gangs, drugs, and domestic violence. Gala and Charles both felt that the new house and neighborhood were worth working as hard as they had to.

Charles was really frustrated with his inability to provide more money for them. He was already working all the overtime that his place offered. All that he had was a high school education, and his diploma was more of a testament to his survival than it was a preparation for the work world.

Gala, on the other hand, was very smart. She graduated from a college that gave her special business training. Charles thought everything about her was special. She was counting on him now. He just had to find a way to make things work.

All of this made Charles mull over an offer again that one of the guys from his old neighborhood in Englewood had made him. The friend worked as a bouncer for a night club. The pay was a little better than his current job in building maintenance. The only thing that had held him back was that his friend had also said, "And if you're smart, you can make some more money on the side, like I do!"

Charles guessed that what this statement referred to was selling drugs. He wanted no part of that! The question was, could he take the one job without being sucked into the other?

He knew in his heart that it was just too big of a risk to take. Yet if Gala didn't get another job soon, he might have to chance it. Then he reconsidered with, "No, no way!"

Charles thought about Elsie. He pictured how she had looked earlier that afternoon when he was getting ready to leave for work. He normally would drop her off by his mother, but this time his daughter had another plan in mind. She just stood waiting for him with her coat, hat, and gloves on. In one hand she had a little plastic lunch box with some cookies that Gala had made. On the floor under the other hand was a little special TV that she could also play some kiddy videos on. It had been a present from Gala's mom.

When Charles saw her just standing there waiting he asked, "Hey, what's with the TV? You know grandma has one at her place."

She answered back directly, "I'm going to work with you so we can see baby Jesus in the manger with his mommy Mary and daddy Joseph!"

Charles then realized what was going on in her little brain. About a week earlier during some quality weekend time off, Charles had sat with Elsie and answered a seemingly unending list of questions about Christmas. Gala was out Christmas shopping so there was no way to shift the answer-giving to her.

Elsie had two areas that she kept coming back to with her questions. One was angels and the other was the manger scene. In an effort to help her to visualize the latter, he suggested that he could take her to see a full-size manger scene that he had spotted from the train. She took this offer to heart and waited each day anxiously for the outing to take place.

The only problem with all of this was that work had been so hectic since then that the time just flew by. Poor Charles forgot to make the visit happen. Now Christmas Eve was here, and Elsie was accepting no excuses.

Rather than break his promise, Charles tried to conceive of a scheme. He knew it was too late to take Elsie to the manger scene before work, so it had to be after. There wouldn't be time enough though for him to go to his mother's house where Elsie would be when work ended and then come back with her on the train to the manger display.

He had worked overtime a couple of nights and observed that after one A.M. the lights illuminating the manger scene were shut off. He guessed that they had them on a timer. This meant Elsie had to be with him when he left work and that meant she had to come to work with him.

After considering all of this, what puzzled Charles was that Elsie had guessed the outcome from the get-go. She said she would watch her videos while her daddy worked, and then he would keep his promise.

The plan came together when Charles realized that there was a safe spot to put Elsie at his workplace. The boiler room was clean and warm, and most importantly, on the second shift he controlled the key to the door. The room was right near the shop, and he could check on her regularly. The way the room was laid out she couldn't go by anything that would get her into trouble. The boilers and all the support equipment were only accessible from a mezzanine, and she wasn't big enough to pull down the ladder that was used to access it.

He also wasn't worried about the other two guys on the shift finding out. They were regularly given assignments on the building's upper floors. For the most part, Charles would be the only one spending much time in the shop.

Charles' scheme unfolded without a hitch. Well, almost. He had actually forgotten about the battery-powered lights in the boiler room. Thinking Elsie was stuck in a pitch black room was his main motivation for getting the backup power generator on as quickly as he had. He was so relieved to find then that the room had immediately lit back up. Otherwise it would have likely scared her bad and ruined his Christmas thinking about it.

Charles brushed all of this out of his mind. He had to concentrate on his duties. He would do another quick check on Elsie and set about walking his rounds. Being Christmas Eve, it looked to be an easy shift.

He had to first check on a couple of his guys who were fixing an automatic heat system damper in an office on the fourth floor. His next chore was to go up to the sixteenth to see that a water cooler that was worked on by the first shift was also done. He didn't expect either of the inspections to take him long. After that he could come down and do work stocking supplies in the shop store room until the shift ended.

With those items done he could then finally focus on taking Elsie for a short visit to the manger scene and having the next two days off. All week he had been making preparations to ensure that he wouldn't be held over on this night. Hopefully that work would now pay off.

* * *

On a Halsted Street bus going south from downtown, a young couple talked as the vehicle made its regular stops and otherwise provided all the riders with a temporary refuge from the wild winter weather that was developing outside. The windows had fogged up, but these two were too immersed in each other to care.

The male was tall with fair skin and red hair. Even while sitting, his head stood noticeably above those of the other passengers. The girl, on the other hand, was quite short and so he was in a state of constantly looking down at her, and she up at him. The size difference obviously didn't matter to them, based on the affectionate looks on their faces and the singing tones of their voices.

They in fact had a lot to be enthusiastic about. In just two weeks they would be married. The biggest plans for the ceremony and reception had been made and at least on the surface all things were right with their world.

There was just one itsy bitsy little problem. Well actually it was a big bomb ready to go off. The male, who's name was Gerry, had a secret. He had hoped in their outing together downtown that day to find an opening to tell her about it. Unfortunately he never felt right in doing it then, and his time was running out fast.

Finally, when his fiancé's stop was only a few blocks away, he spit it out, "Betty, I've got to tell you something. I've been trying all day, but I just couldn't find the words!"

In response to this she got a look of fear on her face that could have frozen him in place. She asked then in a shaky voice, "Tell me what?"

Recognizing her concern he exclaimed, "Oh no! It's not what you're thinking! I'm not getting cold feet or anything like that!"

She breathed a sigh of relief and punched him hard in the chest while yelling, "Don't you scare me like that!"

In just seconds her eyes welled up, and she started digging into her purse for a hanky. He beat her to it though by giving her his. While doing this he stated sincerely, "I'm sorry, honey! I sure didn't mean to make you cry!"

It took her about half a minute to recoup, but finally she asked him while fighting back a sob, "So what is it then that's so darned important?"

"I'm going to change jobs."

Again she got a look of fear and bellowed, "Change jobs! What do you mean?"

Set back by the level of her concern and the attention that it drew from other passengers he quickly added, "Take it easy honey! It's not the end of the world or something!"

Seeing that she would wait and listen, he continued uneasily with, "Well, you know that I've been driving an ambulance to make extra money, and I've been going to classes to get my EMT!"

"Yes, and you told me you wanted to do that as a hobby!"

"Well, that's the problem; I don't want to do it part-time anymore!"

Betty sighed and in a tone of relief said, "Well that's ok, if you don't want to do it. You've got a good job as a maintenance foreman. That's the important one!"

"No, you don't understand! I don't want to work in maintenance anymore. It's just not for me. I want to be a paramedic full time. That's what I really want to do!"

Betty thought about this for a second but saw her corner was fast approaching and stated with frustration, "Oh no, I've got to get off!"

"I'll come with you. We have to finish talking about this!"

So they exited the bus together but found the blowing ice too difficult to shield while in the open. Gerry took her hand, and they ducked into a gangway between two buildings. While blocking the wind from her, he said, "Look, honey, you've just got to trust me with this! You know that I'm a hard worker. I'll make this paramedic job work well for us!"

Betty became preoccupied with rubbing water and film off her glasses but after finishing that answered, "I do trust you Gerry, but when is this all going to happen? Can't you wait until after the wedding?"

"It can't wait, honey! There's an opening for a full-time driver now. They told me if I do this while I finish getting my training they will make me a paramedic. I've got to give them an answer tonight! Otherwise there's another guy that wants the job!"

After a long silence, Betty finally said, "Well if that's what you really want to do!"

Gerry hugged her, and they shared a long embrace, after which Betty asked, "But when will you tell them at your other job?"

"I'm going to tell my boss tonight!"

"Tonight? Won't he be mad?"

"No, I warned him a few months ago that I might be doing this!"

To that Betty got another angry look and punched him again but this time with two hands while exclaiming, "You told your boss then, but didn't tell me?"

Gerry hugged her as much to stop her little attack than anything else while replying, "Listen to me, honey, would you! I couldn't tell you then! I wasn't sure, and we were just beginning to make all of our wedding plans. I didn't think you could handle it! You were already near cracking with all the decisions that we had to make!"

To this she replied after thinking for a moment, "I guess you're right. That would have been a bad time!"

But suddenly she added, "No, Gerry, this is no good!"

Now it was Gerry worrying if she was calling things off, but she added, "We can't have secrets from one another! No matter how I would have reacted, you should have told me! We have to work things out together!"

"I know you're right, now, but I just couldn't see it then. I'm sorry, honey. I really am!"

"And I'm sorry too!"

"You're sorry for what? That we're getting married?"

"No, that's stupid! What I'm trying to say is that I kind of got a secret of my own!"

"What kind of secret?"

Now it was her turn to calm him down. She replied, "Take it easy, would you! It's just that you have to let me help you."

"Help me with what?"

It took her a few moments to gather her thoughts and then she answered with, "Well, remember when you told me that you didn't want your wife to have to work? The reason you gave was that your mom left you and your brother alone too much when you were little, and you got into a lot of trouble, remember?"

"Yes, I remember that! That's still the way I feel!"

"Well, I agree with you for when we have children but there'll be other times when my working will help us do the things we want to do! Like now for instance!

You know you won't get paid as much being a full-time ambulance driver, but we're going to have a lot of expenses. It wouldn't be responsible for us when we're just starting out to already be borrowing money! I'm very capable of working, and I would just die of loneliness if I was stuck in an apartment all day. Don't you see? We need to help each other!"

After taking this in, Gerry answered, "I never thought of things the way you put it. I was scared that if you started working, you wouldn't want to stop!"

"I'll stop for important things like having a family! I know how much that means to you, and I feel the same way."

Hearing this, he just looked at her lovingly, smiled and said, "I guess that I need to show that I can trust you too!"

"Uh-huh!"

For several minutes then before departing, the young couple continued to cling to each other tenderly in the dark.

* * *

On yet another bus, this one heading north on its way to downtown from the south side, an older well-dressed black man peered out the windows at the passing scenery. He was considering how he loved the city in all of its views. Whatever the season, the weather or time of day, he immersed himself in the grand variations of its detail. Somewhere inside him a poet sought to rise out and put words to the feelings that his city world provided:

You horn of people plenty
Please grant me a moment
To see you now just right

So I can fully embrace
The fine portrait you paint
With a city dweller's delight

To me you look splendid
In any gown you put on
In the white of winter
Or black of night

The warmth of your summers
The enthusiasm of fall
The hope of spring
When finally in sight

I thrive on your energy
A fan and transcriber content
To fly with your wind so free

Your wonder can't be contained
By snow sleet or rain
They just come for the ride, like me

Jim Smithers was a happy fellow, reinforced by the fact that it was Christmas time, his favorite season of the year.

There was so much to see, like the always beautiful tree at the Daley Center, the Christmas parades and the lighting of Michigan Avenue. Many buildings downtown were decorated, including his own. There were plays to suit the season, and Christmas carols being played on the radio. All of this and more served to rejuvenate his soul.

Rejuvenation, now that was a process often needed when he considered the living conditions of his neighborhood and of so many others in the city. And when he allowed himself to focus, the core of the problem always came down simply to this, *'Ignorance, poverty, the lack of security, and drugs'*

He remembered vividly how things all started to come apart in the late 60s. Drugs were flowing as free as Lake Michigan water while the misguided youth clamored to experience its so-called magical powers. If it was magic, however, it was the fuel of a curse. Never in his life had Jim seen so many folk intentionally waste their lives.

The demand for the curse was overwhelming. It flabbergasted him that the kids who had fought the entire concept of capitalism and its supply and demand managed to create for themselves and all the rest of the ignorant masses the beginnings of the largest and most evil market that had ever existed in our country.

Every market needs its appropriate share of suppliers and sellers. With the great demand the need grew larger and larger. It had become an industry, a very serious compilation of competitive cutthroat powers.

At first the natural handlers were the mob. They had cut their teeth on booze –smuggling during the Prohibition Era and so their underworld schemes proved to be invaluable. But just like the great Chicago stock yards that once seemed invincible, but were in time replaced by yards out west closer to the cattle sources, the mob was replaced by cartels of those that actually grew the plants from which the drugs were derived. And so the smartass kids that promoted the drugs initially would learn another fundamental of big business, the desire to eliminate the middle man.

Every business that wants to survive in the long run needs an army of agents to intermix with the clients, giving them a kind of a personal attention while they seek to protect their market territories. And so there was a need for those who didn't mind taking the risks associated with an underworld business.

How about the kids that started it all? No, they didn't have what it took. They wanted to use the drugs but being part of the distribution chain got a little too scary for them. They could just get out of it all by running back home to their rich parents while pretending that they had nothing to do with the drug's evil outcome.

Who then might I ask you, fit the bill of the drug suppliers better than street gangs? They were already made up of desperate uneducated kids, many of whom were already hopped up on drugs. They were constantly being told by misguided parents and the stars of their culture not to conform. After all, the new drug sellers were still promoting their products as the rich kids had. These drugs will loosen your inhibitions and free your spirit from the lashings of a rigid society.

So little armies and then larger ones were created out of uninhibited gangs with members that would do just about anything to attain and maintain their status. That included a long list of varied skills they developed like killing, maiming, scaring, torturing, bullying, threatening, raping, kidnapping, and well, you get the idea.

And just to make sure that a continuous source of the combatants was maintained, the gangs started to indoctrinate kids into their evil culture from the youngest ages. Those that chose to take the more civilized path of the folk outside the ghettos would have their minds changed by whatever level of intimidation and cruelty was necessary. If killing them is all that would work, then so be it! That was the world that Jim went home to each night.

He worked desperately to recover from the despair inflicted by these realities. Somehow, someway there just had to be an escape. Should he move away? If things got too hard he just might have to! He couldn't help but conclude though that the problem is here and so must be the answer!

He wouldn't allow himself to fall into the trap that so many of his neighbors had. They just learned to live with the evil, to look the other way, to hide inside their houses that then became their prisons. Their perspective was, "Why fight what you can't beat?"

But somehow he managed to recoup some hope. He just wouldn't give in. So with his job he worked to establish some connections in various groups, organizations, and churches. He clung to whatever would give even an inkling of promise. That is when God gave him a revelation. A fellow he talked with on a bus one day just blurted out something about an organization he had heard of recently. He said that they helped poor kids get real schooling without the influence of the gangs.

Jim's first reaction was that the group had to be a small-scale operation. Who would have the resources to contend with all the monstrous forces that they would be fighting against? But he took the bait! The concept was so rational that he couldn't help being drawn to it.

Well, he surely wasn't disappointed. In fact he was overwhelmed by the promise of sanity that this organization provided. To his amazement, it was no small effort. They operated over 70 schools in the city's most-depressed areas. Then he found that they were not just a large effort. They were a resounding success with the children attaining remarkably good test scores. Most of them advanced through the higher levels of school and even into colleges. How, he wondered, could such a well-run organization be kept under the radar? In his mind it was the city's best-kept secret. He thought it appropriate that it was named after the city of big shoulders.

Jim then became a man with a mission. All of his available free time would be dedicated to finding ways to participate in this beautiful, magnificent, terrific scheme. God had given him a resurgence of hope, and he fell in love with his city all over again.

An integral part of Jim's nature was being inquisitive. This led him to intentionally use different bus routes to get to work even if it meant going far out of his way. Today he was taking the easiest route though because of the holiday. It was the Racine bus that twisted all around on various streets heading north and east until it arrived downtown.

He liked the special character of this route. He had been traveling on it around the old Union Stockyards even before they were closed down back in '71. In fact, he had been taking these buses on and off since the 1960s. He could see on his trips that there were a few landmarks of the yards still standing, like the remnants of the International Amphitheater, the Exchange Building, and the old limestone gate.

Jim remembered watching for signs advertising different events put on at the Amphitheater like the auto shows, circuses, and conventions. He had, in fact, been on a bus heading home the night of the start of the 1968 Democratic Convention. This thought though, always brought with it sad memories of Martin Luther King and Bobby Kennedy. He was filled with hope and didn't want to dwell long on those sad events.

His natural talent was digging through the details of his work. After years of varied job experiences, he had also developed a pretty good view of the big picture. Unfortunately that skill didn't come soon enough for him to realize that he was letting an important facet of life pass him by.

Jim loved people of all types, including his fellow workers, women and children, and even strangers on the street. If he had only reached out for a mate he could have enjoyed life much more. He had kept putting it off with the rationale that he needed to have his career all wrapped up in a fine box with a bow before committing to anything else. Now he felt that he was too old, and marriage had just passed him by.

He had certainly come a long way as far as his career was concerned. It all started out when he was just seventeen years old. Having answered an ad for a maintenance job in the same building that he worked in now, he was disappointed to find that they wanted a man with previous experience. They would however offer him a starting position as a janitor. The job held a stigma that he found difficult to accept, but his desire to work in one of the big buildings downtown overcame it.

At first, his was a trek of slow progression, but he would never have to take a step back. When a position opened in the maintenance storeroom to receive and stock materials, he jumped at it. Then another job finally opened a few years later inspecting fire protection equipment like the extinguishers and hoses that were on each building floor. In time another position became available as a millwright trainee with the maintenance department. He did that too.

Jim didn't stop there though. When training was offered for electrical work, he was the first one to sign up. He continued his education with boiler room classes, and he worked hard and long to pass the test to become a stationary engineer.

With the credentials he had amassed over the years, Jim became a logical candidate for management. He moved through the various levels of assistant foreman, foreman, and shift superintendent. As time went on a couple of these positions were eliminated or modified as part of cost-cutting measures, but Jim had always managed to keep a step or two in front of the changes.

The last and final level he achieved was building superintendent. It was as far as he could go. The position reported directly to the building's board of directors. He was not only ultimately responsible for all of the building services but also for the entire annual budget. It was no small sum. It was no small accomplishment.

Yes, Jim had come a long way. From at least the perspective of time, the building had been his life. In a few years he would be eligible to retire. He wondered what he would do then. For the time being though he would continue to delight in the world that unfolded around him. His mind worked hard on anything that appeared new or different. There was little that he considered too mundane.

By example, one day while on a bus he fixated on a little old woman pulling a metal wire-frame shopping cart on two wheels. He wondered, "Now where might she be going with that? Perhaps she intends to go grocery shopping. If that's the case though, isn't the shopping district behind her? The cart is empty!"

After contemplating the situation further he thought, "If it was thirty years ago, she could be coming back from having returned a couple cases of empty pop bottles, but not now."

"Maybe she forgot her money and that's why she's in such a hurry to get back home or maybe the cart was busted, and she is bringing it back from where it was fixed."

"She might have lent it to someone and got tired of waiting for them to return it, or maybe she is borrowing it herself!"

In any case this is the way that Mr. James Smither's mind would operate as he enjoyed his daily travel to and from downtown Chicago.

On this particular day's ride to work he caught sight of a lad that was no stranger to him walking on Archer Avenue. In earlier days that was not the case. He had noticed back then that the boy always walked kind of slow. He had a book-bag hung on his back and that seemed to bend him over a little. When he first noticed the boy's slow gait, Jim wondered, "Perhaps he's just not in a hurry for some reason."

He pondered the boy further with, "Is his home a hell instead of a haven? Then again he might just be immersed in a world of imagination that unravels out of sync with the movement of his feet."

One day after one of those observations, Jim was quite surprised to see the boy look right back at him as the bus veered around some parked cars and swooped in for a stop. He broke into a most wonderful smile and waved. Jim returned the wave instinctively, but then wondered, "Was he looking at me?"

He turned to the front and the rear of the bus and could see that all the other seats on his side of the bus were empty.

For the rest of the day the image stuck with him. Finally after retracing a number of different encounters, he managed to place the youth. It was at his business Christmas party. He was in fact the son of one of the vendors that serviced his building.

The boy had been at the party with his parents. His father had walked the boy all the way across the ballroom that had been rented for the affair. He then introduced his son to Jim in the following way, "Mr. Smithers, this is my son Jeff. Jeff, this is Mr. Smithers, a man with a good heart. He's the one who gave me the chance to start my life over again!"

The young fellow stepped up close and put out his hand. When Jim received it with his own, the lad smiled large and stated in a most friendly manner, "Thank you, Mr. Smithers. Thank you so very much!"

Jim responded graciously, and the boy and his father then turned and went back to their table.

Jim couldn't help then but to reflect on the situation that had led up to this. In the summer of that past year, the boy's father, a Robert McCall, had stopped Jim one day as he entered the building where he worked. Robert said, "Sir, I heard through some sources that you might be looking for someone to wash the windows on this building!"

"I am indeed! Do you represent a firm that handles high work?"

"I work privately but can handle all the details. If you like, I can show evidence of several of the buildings I have worked on downtown, some in this same area."

Jim was pleased with hearing this and set up an appointment for the man to come and meet with him. As the building superintendent, Jim was in charge of all the services that needed to be done each day to keep the tenants satisfied. These were high-powered financial firms that paid big leases and therefore had equally large expectations.

At the appointment, Jim was very impressed with Robert's knowledge of high-rise window washing. It should be said though that the circumstances that heightened Jim's interest were based on an urgent need.

Sometime earlier, one of the buildings nearby had serious problems with pieces of cornice work breaking away from the building and plummeting down to the sidewalk and street below. It was a relatively new problem for the buildings that utilized these architectural flourishes. Since these structures were in the neighborhood of a hundred years old, there wasn't a lot of information available as to why this had suddenly started to happen.

Naturally, the safety implications of the phenomena were huge. Lawsuits would abound if pedestrians were hit by the falling objects. Critical injury or death could be expected. A variety of building owners were then forced to deal with rectifying the problem and also restudying the insurance they purchased to otherwise protect their interests.

A related problem came to light. The window-washing service companies that were used by these same building owners were concerned about their own liabilities. They couldn't be hoisting equipment and men on the sides of these buildings if in the process there could be falling objects. There would be questions like, "What, in fact, made the pieces come loose? Was it normal deterioration, or did they come loose because of the window-washing procedures?"

This became such a questionable process that the brunt of the contractors that did the window washing refused to work on the buildings that could have cornice work falling. I apologize for this long explanation, but it was necessary because Jim's building included cornice work that was considered suspect despite the fact that none had fallen.

There was then a lengthy period during which the windows of Jim's building were not cleaned. At first the tenants showed a degree of flexibility on the subject. In time though, they started making threats that their contracts were being violated, and Jim knew that he needed a solution fast. It was at this point that Robert McCall had come on the scene.

As far as Jim was concerned, all he needed was verification of Robert's past work, and he would hire him. Unfortunately this check revealed that Robert's last date of doing a window-washing project had been over two years earlier. This sent up a red flag, and Jim called Robert in for a second interview.

To Jim's disappointment, Robert admitted having been in prison for that period. That's when Robert asked if he could explain what happened. Jim agreed but only as a matter of being considerate. At that point, though disappointed, he had already decided against using him. In his building, security was a top priority!

Robert explained how his experience with the high work had put him in a position to watch the business habits of the people in the buildings that he worked on. They would pretty much ignore him when he worked just outside their offices. One day he watched as a well-dressed fellow removed a painting from a wall and revealed a safe behind it. What the man didn't realize was that Robert wore special goggles that could be switched to several levels of magnification. He used these during his work breaks to get detailed views of nearby buildings. As a hobby he would draw sketches of various high-rise elevations.

When saying this, Robert showed Jim several of the renderings he had completed. Jim could see that Robert was a master at capturing the effect of changing light on a building. He was quite impressed with his work.

The story Robert told unfolded further with his using his special glasses to capture the numbers used to open the safe. He explained how he had let greed overtake him. A plan was hatched to break into the office after the occupant left in the evening. It was summer at that time so Robert had a couple of hours of natural light to help him implement his scheme.

Robert had a helper in his window-washing endeavors. The man was a Native American named Phillip Birdtree. Phillip was a big man who pretty much did everything Robert asked as long as he was paid in cash each week. He wasn't much for communication though. In the ten years Robert had known him, Phillip had never put together a sentence of more than four words. The only personal business that Phillip saw to was his own.

When other contractors would ask Robert about Phillip, he would say, "Well, if I was the Lone Ranger, he would be my Tonto. That's about all I can tell you!"

It was because of their long and steady relationship that Robert felt safe going forward with his thievery right in front of Phillip. Afterward he would show him what he had stolen and share it with him. He was already thinking ahead to other jobs that he could pull off.

On the evening that Robert planned the heist, things went as planned. Robert used a glass cutter to remove a square of glass from a window frame and slipped easily into the office. This he intended to replace and then glaze from the outside. It would be difficult then for others to detect how access was made. He moved quickly across the office to reach his objective. It didn't take long, and the safe was open. To Robert's dismay, however, he found it empty.

When he finally shook himself out of the shock of this disappointment, Robert turned to yet another. The hanging scaffold he had come off of to get into the office was not there. He ran to the window and looking out and upward saw it moving up near the rooftop with Phillip on it. He yelled out in desperation, "Phillip, come back!"

But the man moved off the platform to the rooftop and that was the last Robert saw of him. Robert paused his speaking and in an effort to interject some humor into the situation added, "Yes, I imagined afterward hearing Phillip say, 'Not this time Kemsabe!'"

Jim couldn't help but smile, and Robert added, "Yep, the newspapers had a ball with it! 'High Rise Man Gets His Comeuppance' That office was locked from the outside. All I could do then was to wait in that room with the glass gone from the window.

"I would find out later that there were motion detectors in the room and that I had tripped an alarm. Security had the police waiting outside the office door when they opened it.

The group was all smiles as they assessed what I had been up to. Unfortunately the judge didn't find it all to be very funny. I was given two years in prison."

Robert then made a plea to Jim by saying, "Mr. Smithers, I did something really stupid and paid my debt to society. For two years I was away from my wife and son and believe me, I learned my lesson!"

"When I got out, I made a promise that I would never let them down again. I just need one opportunity to do the high work again, but the big outfits won't take a chance on me. They all know though that I'm really good with the window cleaning. If one place gave me a chance, the others would too!"

Somehow Jim changed his mind. He gave a contract for washing his building windows to Robert and the job followed quickly and was done very well. When it was finished, Robert's prediction came true. He had requests from two of the city's biggest contractors to come work for them. They were totally impressed with how he safely approached working on a building that had the questionable cornice work.

Looking back, Jim wondered what it was that made him change his mind. He had been moved by Robert's plea, but it was in fact something else. Having looked at the renderings that Robert had made, he realized that this was not a man destined to be a thief. The drawings exposed a talent and with it, a bit of Robert's soul. What it told Jim was that there was something in the man that would make him flourish if given the chance.

CHAPTER THREE

Cut Clean

*H*aving temporarily dodged behind a building wall for some relief from the onslaught of blowing sleet and snow, Julie, Stash's wife, was immersed in a state of remorse. She knew by then that her scheme of sending Stash and the baby first to see her father had been a bad one. She had worried beforehand that if she had just appeared with no warning that he might refuse to see her. What she had counted on was Stash working things out. He was so good with people! Why though didn't she confess to him what was going on? Why had she been so stupid... stupid and stubborn?

Now she was in an awful dilemma. She thought, "I never stopped to consider how unsure Stash was of the city. He's a farm boy at heart, totally out of his element. He and little Johnny are probably lost and who knows what happened to dad?

"And who were those two men? Why was the one bleeding? Did they break in? Why would anyone break into dad's shop? There's nothing that valuable in there. They didn't look like robbers. The two of them looked old and well dressed like maybe they were businessmen. But why were the books thrown all about? The door was busted, and the one was bleeding! Were they fighting? Oh, God, this is too much to deal with! I'm going out of my mind!"

Determined not to dwell on these thoughts, she adjusted her coat, scarf, and gloves for another fight against the elements. The snow was starting to accumulate in places where the wind couldn't remove it. Any vertical flat surface in the path of the snow's fury was coated by the icy wet stuff. She found it more difficult to advance and after only a half block or so, sought out cover in a building doorway.

As she entered she could see the stationary form of another person. It was thin and appeared to be a black woman. Closer inspection revealed that she was quite young and not at all dressed for such an outing. She had a lightweight coat that cut above the knee and open-toe style patent leather shoes. She wore no hat or scarf or gloves.

It was obvious to Julie that the girl had lost control, just shivering while her teeth chattered. Instinctively, she moved close to the child and hugged her. While doing this she said, "My Lord, sweetie, what are you doing out in this storm dressed like that?"

The girl stopped her chattering for a moment to say, "I did...didn't think this would happen!"

"Well, honey, it's obvious you need to get inside somewhere warm. You're going to catch pneumonia!"

The girl just nodded, and Julie asked, "Which way are you headed?"

"Train station..."

"Well so am I, honey, so we'll go together, ok?"

The girl just nodded again. After watching the weather a moment, Julie added, "Here, you need these things more than I do!"

She took off her scarf and gloves, helped the girl put them on and told her, "Look, honey, it's not going to get any better while we're waiting here, so how about we huddle together and get moving. Union Station is just a couple of blocks away!"

Following this plan they still had to seek shelter every half block or so, but in each case Julie got them started again. When they finally got the station in sight, the young girl shrieked, and they both rushed to it as fast as the weather and the last street crossing would allow.

Once inside the doors they just stood there absorbing the warmth and cover that the large space offered. After a few moments of this Julie suggested that they seek out a bench, and they had little trouble finding an empty one because of the time of day.

Julie panned the room, hoping to spot Stash and her baby but was disappointed. When it was clear that the young girl had thawed out sufficiently, Julie asked her, "What's your name, honey?"

"It's Wilma, Wilma Jackson. Thank you so much for helping me! I thought I would freeze into a pole in that doorway! It was so nice out when I came down this morning. I never thought it would get like this!"

"You're not alone with that, Wilma. I got caught with my pants down today too!"

Wilma smiled, and Julie added, "Are you on your way home, I hope?"

"Well, when my momma gets here."

"Oh, does she work downtown?"

"No, she's coming here to get me"

Julie noticed a little tear forming in her eye and asked, "What's the matter, honey?"

It took the girl a moment to recover and she said sadly, "She's mad, she's really mad!"

"How come she's mad? What happened?"

"I wasn't supposed to come down here, and I spent all my money, so she has to come and get me!"

"Oh, I see, and why was it you did that?"

"Well, every year we come here together on Christmas Eve. It's our one special thing! But she told me this time we couldn't."

Julie waited for her too expand on this but she didn't. So she probed with, "There must be a reason for your mom's decision!"

"Not a good one! Not a reason to spoil our special Christmas outing. We've been doing it since I was four years old! We go to Fields, well, it's Macy's now. Anyway, we look at the window decorations. Then we eat lunch in the Walnut Room by the big Christmas tree. After that we get an ice-cream sundae and then look all around the store to see what's new. Each year, I pick out one special present as long as I don't go over the amount that she told me!"

Taking all this in, Julie said, "Well, that sounds very nice. I can see why you would look forward to such a fun tradition. You haven't told me though, how come your mother didn't do it this year?"

"She said that she didn't have the money! The only thing that's different though is she would have to get a sitter for my baby sister!"

"Well, how old is your baby sister?"

"She's three-weeks old!"

"Just three-weeks old! That's pretty young to be bringing out on a day like this, don't you think?"

Julie caught herself and thought about her own little Johnny. She got a scattered look and exclaimed, "Here I am saying that to you and my own little baby is out there someplace! I should be horsewhipped! What the heck was I thinking?

"I'm sorry, Wilma, I'd like to talk with you more, but I've got to find a phone."

"That's ok, my momma should be here soon."

She pointed while adding, "I think there are some public phones over there."

Julie squeezed her hand and gave her a kind look while adding, "Take it from me, honey. I lost my mom for a long time, and I would have given anything to have her back. Your's sounds like a nice person to me. I'm sure she'll replace this outing with something else. Just because you have a baby sister now doesn't mean that she's stopped loving you!"

With that she smiled and turned in the direction of the phones. Soon she was fishing for some change in her purse and dialing. All she heard was a recorded message saying, "There's no response to your call. At the tone, please leave a message."

She recorded, "Stash, this is Julie. I'm at the train station. If I leave for any reason, I'll tell you where I'm going. Please just stay somewhere out of the weather, anywhere that Johnny will be warm!"

* * *

Back at the shop, Horace had been struggling for a while trying to cover the door opening. He had finally managed to make some progress after finding a roll of clear packaging tape. He used this to fasten the two poster boards together and taped the assembly in place around the door opening periphery. His main difficulties had been with tearing the tape and keeping each piece from folding and sticking together as he tried to apply it.

It had become clear to him that the wind gusts would eventually blow off the large patch if he didn't reinforce it. He looked around the shop and found a few old yard sticks in a barrel. He taped these in several places across the back of the poster board. The tape was very sticky, and it appeared that the patch would hold.

Horace became quite satisfied with himself. It only took a few minutes for there to be a noticeable change in the room's temperature. Wherever the heater was located, it was doing a bang-up job. In the meanwhile, he had grabbed a broom that he had seen in back by the long counter. He set about sweeping the glass on the floor into a pile next to the wall. He was in no hurry to help Matt with the glass in his hands. There was an uncomfortable feeling that came from being around the man that had been caused by their earlier verbal exchanges.

It suddenly occurred to Horace, "The baby, I haven't checked the baby! If he rolls off that table!"

He rushed across the room and found to his relief that the little bundle was still in place.

The infant just stared up at him with a content look and Horace thought, "Your father was right. You are a good little tyke, aren't you?"

He looked over and saw Matt fumbling about and moaning repeatedly as he was trying himself to remove the glass shrapnel. Horace approached him saying, "Here now, I'll do that!"

Matt looked up at him momentarily with a glare but was otherwise unresponsive. Horace quickly grew impatient and stated indignantly, "Well, do you want my help with that glass or not?"

To which he added, "It makes no difference to me!"

Matt held a hand out to give him the tweezers and kept it there with the palm up. Horace grasped it and started to manipulate the tool as Stash had. After about twenty minutes of mining for glass and dropping it with a tinkle into the ornate dragon ashtray, Horace stopped and said, "That's all I can find in that one. There may be some tiny fragments yet, but the blood staining makes it difficult to see."

After a final inspection he added, "I'll start on the other in a little while. I have to straighten my back out. I'm not used to bending down this way. In any case I have to check on the baby."

Matt made no comment. The fact was that he needed a break but wouldn't have admitted it. A couple of times while Horace worked on him he had felt nauseated. He had a hard time dealing with pain, especially the acute variety. And blood, that was something he had a real problem with. Now he was full of the stuff and all he could do was lean his head back and close his eyes.

He held a dark secret, and his mind was whirling with how to deal with it. It seemed that a force was working against him. He wouldn't be stopped though. His whole life had become focused on one objective, and he wouldn't let himself stop until it was over. After that nothing else would matter.

Horace stood staring down at the bald-headed baby and thought, "He or she must be pretty young. No correct that. Stash called him Johnny. Well that's settled, it's a little boy. It can't be more than a couple of months old."

He couldn't imagine however, why anyone would take an infant out into such awful weather. Another consideration came though, "I guess it was pretty mild at mid-day. They probably came down right before all the hell broke loose. This was one of those times that the weathermen were sure caught off-guard and everyone else in the city with them!"

He knew how the so called experts would explain it, "Must have been a lake-effect storm!"

It was a much-used expression in Chicago to describe unexpected snow.

He thought, "Well, Stash did say that the weather suddenly changed. Yes, that's what he indicated, wasn't it?

"He comes across as a sensible fellow. Still, it seems pretty foolish that he and his wife separated, especially with his not knowing his way around."

The baby just lay there looking up at him. He tried moving his finger above it to get its attention. Seeing no reaction, he surmised that it was too young to focus. He wondered what he would do if it started to fuss. Old memories warned him that it was just a matter of time. His own child had been a good baby too, but all of them fuss or cry sooner or later. That was something his wife had told him one day when his daughter had suddenly started with an outburst.

He remembered how he had never changed a single diaper. This he had left to his wife. Back then she used the ones made of cloth. Eventually he had seen how they were replaced by throwaways. He had to admit that the new kinds advertised on television were pretty well designed, with their sticky tabs replacing the safety pins. He had trouble opening and closing those pins with his big stubby fingers. Perhaps he would have tried a change or two if the new style diapers were available when his daughter was a baby.

He quickly admitted to himself though, "Probably not."

His wife was the caregiver; he was the breadwinner. When his daughter cried, he left the room. He found the crying to be so disconcerting.

"Well, why should I have stayed for it? It's not like she was really sick or something!"

The truth was that he didn't help much in those times either. He just couldn't comfort his daughter by holding her the way his wife could. She would tell him, "Horace, you're too stiff! She senses your awkwardness. Sit down with her and relax!"

This was something he really needed from his wife, her frankness. She always got right to the point. He could quickly assess where she stood on a subject. It gave him the opportunity to react. It was in fact the key thing that had attracted him to her. She was the polar opposite of his mother!

He regretted this analogy immediately. It was a fire starter. He tried to blank out his thoughts, but it was no use. He fell slowly, drifting down, down into a deep abyss. There was no escaping it. Thoughts flushed out in batches. He had gone to this dark place so many times before. Now he was swimming in it.

His parents had provided no warning. There were no discussions, no arguments, and no fights. Nowhere in the whole of his memory could he find a reason and oh-so hard he had tried. Father being gone was no clue! He had done that regularly. His mother showed no signs of it upsetting her. Everything was so controlled, so tempered, so seemingly civil!

One day when he was nine years old, she woke him up early to say, "Horace, you're not going to school today. There is something I have to do!"

Startled, he opened and closed his eyes a couple of times while trying to focus. Then having had a moment to absorb what she had said his reaction was, "This could be a good thing!"

He had only missed school one other time that he could remember. That was when he had his tonsils out. It was so nice then to stay home for a couple days while being pampered by his grandmother. In fact it was the only time he could remember the kind old woman coming to their house.

She was great, letting him do anything he wanted. He had heard kids at school talking about listening to some neat radio shows, so that was his request. She let him freely turn the radio's control knobs. It was so fun to explore all that it offered. There were so many fun shows like Amos & Andy and Fibber McGee & Molly. Even the talk shows were great to listen to with big stars like Bing Crosby, Fred Allen, and Jack Benny.

His mom, if given the opportunity, would have had none of it. Fortunately for Horace she had opted to leave during the day when her mother was there. When she came home in the evening the first thing she did was shut off the radio with him sitting on a chair and listening right in front of it. She told him that it would weaken his mind. People needed to think for themselves, not fill their heads with such a bunch of foolishness. Still, when he visited his grandmother on another day, he couldn't resist the temptation.

He thought, "Well if I'm weakening my mind, I'm just doing it a little!"

On this particular day though, when his mother woke him, his balloon of anticipation burst when she added, "Get dressed quickly now, you have to come along with me."

He quizzed her on where they were going, but she replied with an abrupt, "Never mind about that now, you'll see soon enough!"

Knowing from her tone not to press the subject further, his mind raced to figure it out. While exiting their home he recognized the large limousine waiting in front at the curb. It belonged to grandfather. The man never drove it himself. There was a driver hired just for that purpose.

He thought, "We must be going to see my grandparents. That could be a good thing, especially if mother locks into a long conversation with grandfather. Then I can be with grandmother and who knows what fun things we might do?"

That, he knew would be quite extraordinary. Their visits to his grandparent's home were few. For the most part his mother chose to see her father at his business. It wasn't for the lack of grandmother's asking. Mother just didn't allow for it in her schedule. He remembered one time when grandmother offered to visit in almost a pleading fashion and then showed real disappointment on her face after being turned down. Grandfather, Horace had assessed, shared the same cool and indifferent attitude as his mother.

It became obvious after a few minutes in the limo that they weren't going to the grandparent's house either. He recognized some landmarks. The vehicle was headed toward downtown. He couldn't imagine any reason at all why they would be going there.

It finally occurred to him, "Perhaps we're just passing through!"

He would know if the big buildings came and went. Suddenly a horrific thought came to him, "What if someone died and we're going to the funeral?"

He had been to one of these when his great aunt Hilda passed away. She had been such a bubbly woman the couple of times that he had seen her at family gatherings. He was forced to go up by the open casket when she was waked. This view didn't do right by her. She looked so sullen just lying there.

He thought that experience was very sad. No one seemed to really care that she was gone. All those attending just walked about talking to one another as if she were invisible. Oh, he hoped upon hope that this day's business wasn't a wake or a funeral. He couldn't have possibly guessed that it would in fact be, much worse.

The limousine suddenly rolled to a stop in the heart of the city. The tall buildings dwarfed everything. His eyes were drawn to one across the street, but his mom pulled on his hand. They were soon entering another building nearby through its large revolving doors. He wasn't yet used to these. He worried that somehow he would get caught between the moving part and the curved wall that it slid against. She made him go first, and he was swooped in by the door section pushing against his backside. The first thing he saw after being thrust out was a sign that directed to "Courtrooms." Soon they were in an elevator with a couple other people on their way to the higher floors.

When the elevator stopped, his mother pulled him along briskly through a long hallway. Her motion stopped abruptly when they were next to two large wooden doors. She turned to him then with an oh-so serious glare and leaned down a bit for even more focus while stating, "Horace, now this is important! Pay attention. You will see several people we know in there, my parents, and even your father. There's something very important being settled. There is a man in front called a judge, and he will make the decisions. You must not say anything to disturb what is going on. Do you understand?"

He replied that he did. One thing that he knew as a nine-year-old was to keep his mouth shut when told. The training had been done extremely well. A military drill sergeant couldn't have evoked more fear in his men. He would not let out a peep. It was, after all, one of those adult things. He had no idea why he needed to be in this place anyway and hopefully it wouldn't take very long.

That's what he was thinking when one of the big brown doors swung open in front of him with an eerie groan. Mother walked down the aisle that had benches to each side at her earlier determined pace. He had to practically run to keep up. It was like the times when his bus was late getting to the school and all the kids were running to their respective classrooms under the prompting of the adults waiting for them.

The dark wooden benches in that large room appeared to be empty except for one on the right side at the very front where a couple adults were sitting. He looked to the other side and that's when he saw his father sitting a little forward of the benches at a table. Next to him were two men.

It seemed strange that his father didn't turn to look at him. To the other side he recognized that it was grandfather and grandmother that were in the front bench. Mother stopped there and directed him to sit next to them. They moved over and made a spot for him right at the end while his mother walked forward and was greeted by two men at yet another table.

In a few minutes a white bearded man in a black robe came into the room and everyone stood up. He moved to a chair behind a large desk that sat higher than everyone else. He directed those attending to sit back down and talked for a couple of minutes with another man that stood close by him. The room remained quiet.

After a few minutes of this he looked over at the men sitting by his mother and asked them something that Horace couldn't understand. There was a floor-standing fan running just to the side of the judge, and the hum tended to muffle things a bit. The adults finished their part after which the bearded man talked with the men by his father's table.

There was a repetition of several of these exchanges by the people just mentioned. The bearded man also directed some questions to his mother and father. Horace couldn't understand most of this talk either. All he could make out was hearing several times, "And do you agree…"

But he couldn't grasp what they were agreeing to because of the fan and the tendency of the judge's voice to trail off in each sentence. It was like he didn't have the energy or inclination to hold up his volume.

When this was done the bearded man hit his desk with a little wooden hammer and said something like, "With the matter settled, this hearing is concluded!"

Horace's mother stood up and shook hands with the men by her, and his father did the same with those by him. The grandfather joined the men by his mother and they all shook hands again. All of a sudden then Horace's father turned and walked down the aisle that his mother and he had come in through. Again his father didn't look at him. All he could assume was that he was in a hurry as usual to get to somewhere to do something, whatever that was.

Horace's assessment of that morning's activities in court was simple, "Well, whatever they wanted to do, everyone seems to be pretty satisfied!"

The important thing from his perspective was that it didn't take very long at all! He had actually smiled at the prospect of getting home earlier and maybe even having some time to spend with his friends when they returned from school. With a look of relief on his face, he turned to his side and was surprised to see his grandmother wiping a tear from her eye. He reacted by blurting out, "What's the matter, grandmother? Why are you crying?"

She looked at him, softly took his hand and replied, "Horace, oh, my Horace, don't you know what happened here today?"

"No, not really grandmother, I just guessed that it was some kind of family business!"

"Family business, oh my Lord!"

With that, Horace's mother turned around abruptly and said to her, "Mother!"

Grandfather did the same and added, "Ethyl!"

And there was no more talk. That was the end of it. Horace's curiosity was heightened by this, but he actually didn't find out until several days later what had happened. He said quite casually to his mother one evening, "When father returns, I must show him my grade card from school. I did quite well this term. Don't you think so?"

She just stared at him then with a cold and sinister glare, only made worse by the silence that continued on for an uncomfortably long period. He added in frustration as an effort to break the torturous spell, "Well, don't you think my grades were good? My classmates and teachers thought so!"

She finally answered, "Horace, I can't believe that you fail now to understand what happened in court on Monday!"

He just looked at her blankly wondering what that had to do with his grades. She added soon after in a disgusted manner, "Obviously you do not! Well, let me make it perfectly clear to you. Your father and I have been divorced. If I and your grandfather can manage it, and I think that will be done quite satisfactorily, we will never have to put up with seeing him again!"

With that, Horace was the one left staring. But there was naught but a vast emptiness in front of him! He was stunned, with reality finally coming to light. Mother and grandfather had used the latter's influence to make something awful happen. He no longer had a father! This prompted his reflecting on the day in court, and he had many questions for his father that kept jumping out at him such as, "How could you let this happen without even looking at me? How could you do this? How could you agree to just leave me alone forever?"

In his present adult condition, Horace recalled for perhaps the thousandth time how his father had not really been much fun to be with. The one important thing that the man had offered though was some balancing to his mother's extremes—of which there were many. His father often chose the exact opposite of what she demanded and would somehow manage to get his way.

An example of this was that she would insist that all of Horace's homework be done the night that it was assigned. Horace would try to explain to her that it often wasn't meant to be. Some were weekly or even monthly assignments. Despite that, she wouldn't give in to him and insisted it be settled when his father came home. When his father finally arrived she would demand that her husband adhere to his responsibility to make sure that Horace followed through with his school duties.

Had he accepted the premise of the onslaught, the project would have necessitated a great deal of legwork on his father's part. He would have had to help Horace fetch materials, drive him to the library, and be available to check work as the night went on into the wee hours of the following day. The man wanted no part of this. He insisted that the work be done as assigned. Horace was relieved as mother finally capitulated.

He could not help but remember then, her favorite bitter closing on such a matter, "You may have won this battle, but I will prevail in the end!"

His father gave the threat no value. He just brushed the conflict off as if it were a piece of lint resting on his trousers. Seeing that, Horace did the same.

Now he was stuck with his mother's excessive views. It wouldn't matter whether he got good grades or not. His performance was measured by her obsessive nature and would never be good enough. When his father had been home on the weekends, he got to sleep in, but that luxury was over. She immediately found another learning session for him to attend.

This was added to the piano lessons with no one to play for besides his instructor and dancing lessons with only students as partners. Over time he would have speech lessons, controlled manners exercises, leadership training, business preparations, household management, bank transactions, bookkeeping, classical music appreciation, personal hygiene, abstract art appreciation, architectural reviews, achievement seminars, and college selection. A ton of forced information, not even one little ounce of love!

It was an awful lot to accept and absorb for a nine-year-old. In time the nightmare became an unchanging reality and all he wanted was for it to end. He wondered if a child could get a divorce from his mother.

He yearned desperately for an escape and hoped to somehow get his father's address so that he could plead for help. Despite however having kept a detective-like surveillance of all the mail coming to the house, there had been none from his father. He tried to monitor his mother's banking communications and transactions but these were kept off-limits to him.

It was strange that even at this young age, Horace had his own bank account. You would think, logically, that this would have granted him some independence. But it might as well have belonged to someone else because his mother enforced a countersigning provision. So even that abstract thing, money, which all importance was assigned to by his mother and grandfather, was being denied to him. And so the seed was planted for him to find a way to have it. Only time would tell if he would succeed. He suspected that the key was to be an adult, a person that could release the jaw of his mother's vise.

For that time though, when play should be a child's refuge, Horace was trapped in the cold sterile box that his mother had created for him. His contact with children from the neighborhood was reduced to none as she took captive every morsel of time that would otherwise have been available. The middle and high schools she chose for him fit the mold of her desires. Finally he just gave in to all of it and became the entity that she had willed.

CHAPTER FOUR

Signs of the Past

Almost directly across the street from the antique shop was one that catered to smokers. Most any legal tobacco product that was desired by the diehard breed could be purchased there. Cigarettes by the package or carton, cigars individually or in the box, chewing tobacco in bags and cans, and pipe tobacco too. There were also accessories that were no longer readily available in most department stores, like pipes, lighters, ashtrays and books of matches. Despite the negative stigma attached to smoking, the shop's proprietor had little trouble making all the most popular brands available. The dwindling list of suppliers tripped over each other to have him display their products.

For the holidays, the shop was dressed in the classic red and green. Many products were displayed in special gift wrap with gold, red, silver, and blue ribbons and bows. The shop itself held a most-pleasing aroma that could be enjoyed by customers all yearlong.

The proprietor couldn't care less that some folks walked by and viewed the shop as if it were a great white elephant. It was his business, and it had been his father's business before him. Ironically, when it first opened, the shop was one of the few black-owned businesses in the whole downtown matrix.

Seldom was the store crowded now with clients as in years past, but still there was a regular stream that stopped by. They were pleased that it was open on every day of the week including Sunday.

Occasionally the establishment would be visited by a local politician. The man or woman would typically act indignant with the owner and say something to the effect of: "My good sir, surely you could find better employment than this to serve the cause of humanity! This place is a disgrace to the principles of a good and healthy existence!"

The owner knew, however, that these were hypocrites and their emotional outpourings were all done for show. As long as he kept paying the high taxes assessed on his products, he would likely hold his place in the neighborhood. Well, at least for a while. As far as he was concerned there was not a creature on earth that could devise as many ways of taxing their so-called constituents as a Chicago politician. The proprietor just shrugged this off. Customers told him that they didn't care if smoking was banned from the universe, they would somehow buy their tobacco, one way or another.

He remembered how one of the same haughty politicians that had assailed him, had been shown on TV recently, arm in arm with a group of suits endorsing the latest casino in the state. These people didn't care to respond to the truly community-minded groups that protested against them. They were the ones that claimed that the bought-and-paid-for politicians were just creating more places for well-placed villains to rob old ladies and men of their retirements. No, the politicians knew that casino owners pay taxes too, and they do it in a very large and powerful way.

The proprietor was sure that in time his trade would be eliminated. It was his hope though that he could keep on working till his health failed him. With that he would be satisfied. He had just turned seventy-five years old and might have a couple more left.

It wasn't that he didn't have a conscience, mind you. The results of what tobacco did to users was well understood by him. He couldn't justify his position other than that tobacco sales had been the only means he knew of to survive. It was now ironic that for much of his life the products were considered a natural and wonderful benefit of living. You saw people smoking everywhere then, even in the movies and on television. Cigarettes were a status symbol of sorts. But that all changed and the best thing he knew of to do now was to let the shop die when he did.

The shop owner's name was Ben Simms. At the moment his concern was not with his shop or his own longevity but with the welfare of his friend Frank Fleming. That man, who you should know at this point, owns the antique shop across the street. They are of a similar age and have known each other for some sixty-seven years.

The two also shared the fate of having inherited their businesses. Their friendship however, started before that as they had each grown up in the shops and apprenticed when they were teenagers. Ben had been attracted to all the great old relics that Frank's father's shop displayed in its windows, like swords, helmets, guns, ornate jars, lamps, clocks, oriental rugs, odd furniture pieces, and yes, the books. He loved to sit and read and thought it was wonderful that Frank's father would let him borrow them. It was like a library but much more convenient.

Frank was equally attracted to all the smoking products that were offered just across the street. In a like manner of generosity, Ben's father had given him an old pipe that he claimed was carved by a captain that sailed off the Caribbean islands. He still used and treasured that pipe to this day.

The world erupted while they were young lads with the great tensions of World War II . They shared the anxiety of whether it would continue so long as to pull them into it. It finally ended, and they celebrated with the masses and felt great relief. The Korean War, though, followed soon after, and they both enlisted. The patriotic influence of the printed word and stories told by those returning from the earlier war had a great influence on them.

That was, however, for both of them, the time when they could have taken the reins of their fathers' businesses. Fortunately, they managed to return from the bloody conflict. His friend Frank had come home a bit earlier than he had because of a leg wound. The two then had great worldly experiences to share. They started a ritual of meeting together before and after each day's duties. For a long while their favorite place to opine was Sally's Grill that was located next door to Ben's shop.

The area around their businesses was especially popular in the fifties. The restaurant was almost always full during the day, and on the other side of Ben's place was a barbershop owned by an Italian fellow named Vito Bertucchi. Ben and Vito had arranged for another black man named Alonzo Franklin to run a shoe shine business on the sidewalk in front of their shops. The offerings of each of these businesses turned out to be good for the others in terms of attracting customers.

When the weather was bad they let Alonzo move one of his chairs into each shop, and he had a fellow that worked with him named Sam that manned the second one. Only a short ways down from the front of the mentioned shops, closer to the corner, was a newspaper stand that was run by a woman named Susan Dunn. All of these small business owners were friends and socialized as much as their daily duties would allow.

In those days Frank and Ben were more like family than many who should have been. Both found partners and were married in a few years and in each case they requested the other to be their best man. Their wives would soon each have a child that the proprietors predicted would run their businesses as they had. Neither would however, in the long run.

Ben's boy of the same name joined the army to see the world. He had been enamored with all of the war and travel stories that his father and Frank had told. Sadly, all he got to see was a base in the states where one day he was killed in an accident while out riding his motorcycle on a farm road. Ben grieved for a long time. A few years later his wife Margelie died too, of a rare disease, and he grieved again.

Frank and his wife Deborah named their daughter Julie. For years she was the light of Frank's life and was his main source of strength after his wife left the two of them for greener pastures. That happened when Julie was only six years old.

Frank was sure that Julie would officially take over his shop when she got into her twenties but that milestone had come and went. She also hadn't married though and so Frank held out hopes that she would finally commit to being a proprietor. He reasoned that for all practical purposes she had been like an owner, constantly trying out new selling schemes, arranging and rearranging the stock.

Through all of that, Frank watched her with pride from a distance. She seemed to give him all the signs of liking being there. When she was thirty-one years old, however, things changed drastically for him. Julie's mother came back into her life.

Julie had always been a kind and thoughtful child and when she found out that her mother was stricken with a crippling disease, she left her father and the shop to tend to her needs. At that time her mom lived in a small town in northern Indiana, and Frank thought that Julie might as well have moved to the end of the earth. He had always relied on city buses to travel and never owned a car or even learned to drive.

Frank felt bitter at Julie for leaving him. He insisted that she come back and when she wouldn't, he got so angry that he just washed his hands of her. He told Ben, "She's made her choice now! That's the end of it."

Ben tried over several years to change his friend's mind but with age Frank became more and more stubborn. Fifteen years had passed without Frank ever being willing to see Julie despite many efforts on her and Ben's part. She wanted her dad to come to Indiana because she just couldn't leave her mom, whose condition had slowly worsened. The fact was that Julie had been hurt herself when her father wouldn't accept her helping her mother. Along with that she shared a large share of his stubbornness.

Now Frank's health was failing too and despite Ben's encouragement he still wouldn't call her. This was what had been occupying Ben's mind that day. Until, that is, he started seeing folks going into Frank's shop. His eyes were failing him though, and he just wasn't sure of what was going on.

Ben hoped that a young man that helped him around the shop would come by as he routinely did each evening. The worker's name was Jesse. If he came he would send him over to see what was going on. Unfortunately, it was a long shot, because it was Christmas Eve, and the weather was obviously turning real bad.

He worried, "What if he doesn't come? What will I do then?"

He then even worried about sending Jesse. If something was amiss, he didn't want the young man getting hurt. Jesse had a wife and young daughter of his own. Ben didn't admit it outright, but Jesse had been a real help to him around the shop. He had grown to rely on his assistance more and more, especially since his eye problems had gotten worse.

Ben had seen a light coming through the antique shop door earlier but now it was gone. He had also noticed someone coming out but could have sworn that two people had gone in. To add to the confusion, Frank had not come by to see him that morning. He remembered how he and Frank had agreed a while back that Ben wouldn't cross over the street with as bad as his eyes had gotten.

He wondered, "What if something has happened to Frank? What if he had a heart attack? Maybe that's why those people are in his shop. But there was no ambulance! Wouldn't they have called one?"

Several times he considered going across. Once he even dressed for it, but when he opened his door the wind and rain were blowing very hard. He was a slight man and knew he couldn't manage it. He just didn't know what to do.

Finally he opted to call the police. When he explained the situation, though, they surmised that it wasn't an emergency. They already had their hands full. Despite that, they did take down the address and said that they would send a car when one was available. The dispatcher explained that it could be awhile and asked if he wanted them to send a paramedic.

The policeman quickly added to this in a serious tone that unless Ben really thought someone was hurt that he should not bother the paramedics. They, like the police, were already crisscrossing the city answering calls. Ben didn't know how to answer in light of these conditions and just said that he would call back. This was the state that he was in as the two men and the baby occupied the antique shop and Stash and his wife, Julie, were out in the weather looking for one another.

* * *

When she returned toward the bench where Wilma had been seated, Julie saw that the girl was gone. For a moment she worried about her but soon spotted two people hugging in the distance. She was relieved to see that it was Wilma and her mom. Julie could relate to their situation. Sitting back down she started to reminisce about how she had felt when she was Wilma's age.

As a teenager she had reached a point of wanting some control over her life. All kinds of questions had erupted. One of them was, "Why can't I go and see mom?"

"Maybe she's different now. Maybe she regrets leaving and wants to see me as much as I want to see her! All I have to do is find out where she is. It doesn't matter how far. People can go anywhere by train!"

These thoughts would result in an uproar of sorts around the antique shop. For week's she plagued her dad as well as Ben and Kathleen at the diner, about how she might go about finding her mom. Frank got really upset and tried to put the clamps on the subject, but his attitude only made Julie more determined.

Ben and Kathleen were put into a bad spot because they didn't want to betray their friendship with Frank. That though didn't change their opinion on the subject. They could understand very well what it felt like to miss someone that was lost to them. When the subject of a letter from Julie's mom came up, all hell broke loose.

Julie in her thrash-and-toss-about manner of that time, happened one day to be looking for a pen in the drawer of Frank's desk. When trying to see under piled paraphernalia in the rear compartment, she accidentally pulled the whole drawer out, and its contents spilled to the floor. Amongst these droppings was a letter that had been stuck under the drawer.

Julie picked it up and at first was not interested because it was addressed to her dad. Then she noticed the return address. The name was Dorothy Fleming. It was from her mom! Ordinarily she respected her dad's correspondence and wouldn't have opened it, but she thought mistakenly, "Dad must have missed this, or he would have told me!"

She thought further, "Well, anything from mom has to be meant for me too!"

In this case she was right, but her dad had not intended for her to see it.

The letter read,

Dear Frank,

I'm sure that it must be a surprise to you that I am writing after all these years. I don't blame you if you don't want to read on, but for Julie's sake, I hope that you will. It took me a long time to come to my senses and realize what a fool I've been, but I do now understand that very clearly. I'm not asking for forgiveness, but I do want you to know that I am sorry! I treated you so badly. You did nothing to deserve my running out on you.

I've tried recently to restart my life. When I received the divorce papers a couple of years ago, I figured that you wanted things cut clean. I was somehow given a second chance and met another man. He doesn't measure up to you, but he tries each day to do the best that he can.

I have many regrets, but none larger than what I did to you and Julie. If you hate me I understand, but I think every day of how lost Julie must be at this age without a mom. She must be eleven years old now. It's a difficult time for any girl; I know it was for me. Her body is changing, her needs are changing, and one of those is to have someone to talk about these things with.

At this point while fighting back a tear, Julie stopped reading and thought, "Eleven years old?" and she scanned the top of the page and saw the date.

This made her cry out, "Oh my God, this is two years old!"

She quickly read on through the rest of the note:

Frank, could you see it in your heart to let me meet with Julie? I would do it on any terms that you want. I just don't want her to think that I'm devoid of all feeling for her. That's probably what she thinks now, with the way I left her. She must find out that I do love her and miss her and am so...so sorry! Otherwise she'll carry the hurt with her for all of her life. I can't bear to think that she is feeling lost, the way I did with my own mother. Please Frank, if I could see her and talk to her just once. It's all that I ask.

Sincerely,
Dorothy

Julie folded over and started to sob. This letter meant more to her than anything else in her life. It was like a great weight had been lifted off of her. More than ever she wanted to meet with her mom. She held tight to the letter and the envelope with the return address as if they were the greatest treasures on earth.

When Julie showed the letter to her dad it became obvious that he had seen but not opened it. Having possession of the letter though was enough to overlook her father's awful decision to hide it from her. After she wrote to her mom, and time passed without an answer though, there was hell to pay. Her dander built to yet a higher pitch when Frank refused to read the letter. She had put it right in front of him several times, but he just got up and walked away.

This finally prompted Julie to go two whole months without exchanging a single word with Frank. She would talk to Ben, or Kathleen, or the other business owners in the area. She would even get into lengthy conversations with sellers and buyers and casual visitors. Frank though, might as well have been the plaster on the walls or the dirt on the floor as far as Julie was concerned. That was also the time when she started spending much more of her days with Kathleen at the diner than she did in her dad's shop.

Kathleen and Ben did all they could to break the ice. They staged numerous situations for the two to be forced to engage one another. Unfortunately, Frank himself remained immovable.

Finally one day, as Julie was due to start her first day of high school, things came to a head. Instead of asking Frank for the money she needed, Julie went right to the cash register. He however had already turned toward it to make change for a customer. She started to slam it close, but Frank grabbed and held it at the last moment. Julie continued to push, and Frank reacted by pulling back with all his might.

Having gotten frustrated with the standoff, Julie suddenly let go, and the drawer flew open with Frank hurling backward. He hit his head, ironically, on the old wooden medical cabinet hanging on the wall and went down for the count.

Julie shrieked and bent down over him yelling, "Daddy, daddy, daddy, are you alright?"

She ran to the back room and returned with some smelling salts which she used to revive him. He was groggy and had a knot growing fast on the back of his head but would still have been better off not to say a thing. He did anyway with, "Stupid girl, why in the hell did you do a dumb thing like that?"

Well, you would have thought that an ocean rig had just drilled through to a gusher. She unleashed on him for five minutes straight with all kinds of stored up angst, much of which isn't fit to be written here. In short she couldn't believe he had left the letter unopened, hid it away and never mentioned it to her. In the process he ruined her one chance of seeing her mother. It could be said in the end, and some did, that at least they were talking again.

The wound was deep and never healed right for either of them. What Julie didn't know was that he had in fact read the letter after she had. One of the times she had put it in front of him he came back into the room when Julie was gone. Before then a little hope had rekindled in his heart when he had heard Julie say, "Dad, please! She's trying to apologize!"

He thought for a glimpse of a second that he and Dorothy could get back together. He still loved her. He had never stopped. When he read though that she had remarried, it was like she was leaving him all over again. He couldn't bear it and immediately regretted reading the letter. All he had a mind to do was retreat and wished he could bury himself in a hole and have it all be over. With that, things failed to get back to normal. It took a long while before they would even tolerate one another.

CHAPTER FIVE

A Lifelong Challenge

Horace looked down at the baby, and it seemed so content. He couldn't imagine how it could be, just lying in that one place for so long. Something came to mind from far in the past. He had been in a similar posture staring down at his baby daughter when his wife interrupted his trance with, "Pick her up, Horace, you won't break her!"

He replied, "I just don't feel right, holding her while I'm standing! She's so tiny. I worry that she'll get swallowed up in my arms. I feel like if I moved at all, she could slip through the smallest space and fall!"

His wife just sighed and stated, "You're not going to drop her, Horace, but if it'll make you feel better, sit down in a chair, and I'll lay her in your arms."

He agreed and so that's what they did. She went to great lengths adjusting the baby's position to make sure he was comfortable holding her. This made him feel quite satisfied, and he thanked her. While looking down at the baby, he felt that he was really accomplishing something. It was great to just stare at her angelic little face from such a close position.

That's when something that he thought was quite extraordinary happened. The baby started making little cooing and gurgling sounds, and he felt like she was trying to talk to him.

He looked up for a moment to tell his wife, but she had left the room. It was a wonderful moment, and he could have sat watching and listening to her all day.

As babies often do though, she finally grew uncomfortable. First she started to fidget, and her discontent slowly built into a bout of prolonged crying. Horace looked around desperately for what to do, but Kathleen was still gone. He tried to get up but was sunk down deep into the easy chair. This made him shuffle about from side to side to get into a position from which he could stand. Bewildered and frustrated with the baby's continued crying, he finally managed to rise and grasped tightly to the infant in the process.

Just as he straightened out he focused, and saw his wife standing there smiling. She said calmly, "Here, Horace, I'll take her!"

And he was never so relieved.

It took him awhile before he dared to hold the baby again, but with Kathleen's constant encouragement he did. The sitting position in the chair in their living room was the only place that he would do it.

He would always ask Kathleen first, "You're not going to get too far away are you?"

And she would sigh, but then console him with something like, "No Horace, I will be here to come to your rescue."

He recalled how rescuing him was what Kathleen had done from the very start. They had met in a little diner that had been owned by her mother, Sally Fitzgerald. It was in fact the same restaurant that had been located just across the street from the antique shop.

Horace was attracted to the place by the large assortment of colorful characters that frequented the area. It was such a contrast to the business world that had become the logical extension of his upbringing. He worked on the fifteenth floor of the building that somehow allowed the little antique shop to be a part of its base. That side of the street was otherwise dedicated to all things financial. There was a bank to one side of the shop and a real-estate based law firm to the other. All the above floors were filled with businesses whose owners, partnerships, conglomerates, etc., believed that they made the world go around.

He was soundly planted in that same belief and culture. Still he couldn't help but be amused with how animated the people were that utilized the various little shops and their associated curiosities across the road.

There was one other factor that would eventually bring Horace closer to these common folk. That was a persistent need to satisfy his hunger. Food had grown to be very important to him. He packed it away in large volumes and felt no need to explain the compulsion to anyone.

This inner drive to consume created a predicament in those early days when he was so focused on success. The problem being that it took him too long to walk or even take a cab from his building to the finer eating establishments. He was determined not to let the black mark of being late in returning spoil his fine record. Till this point he had been buying a box lunch in the morning on his way in and eating it in the company cafeteria. The habit was getting old, because the food, by his assessment, was just barely edible.

Lately then, Horace entertained the possibility of taking a lunch at the diner across the street. This was not something he would do in haste. He was truly concerned about the nature of those he would be eating with. If he found that the establishment offered a booth with some privacy and some reasonable choice of entrees, he might then attempt it.

He pondered how he would go about getting a menu. The thought of having the department secretary do that for him was too risky. She couldn't be trusted with a secret and such a story might serve as amusement for his superiors. That select group frequented only the finest restaurants. Unlike Horace, their time spent dining was not a factor. And so he concluded that his method of checking out the diner had to be more clandestine.

One day, in a carefully planned excursion, he overcame his concerns and left for the foreign place. His scheme was to cross at the corner with a crowd, hoping in that way to remain inconspicuous. From there he would casually enter the corner drugstore. He hoped to look out the window and observe any obstacles that might be lurking on the street between him and the restaurant.

Having gone that far, he was surprised and pleased to discover that the diner had an interior access from the drugstore. From an adjoining glass window he could see that the place was not as large as those he was used to frequenting. It did however have booths in addition to some tables. His position put him closest to a long counter with stools that served to separate the kitchen from the main eating area.

He was most happy then to discover a paper menu taped on the glass next to the entry door. There were offerings like meatloaf with mashed potatoes and gravy, fried chicken with egg noodles, spaghetti with meatballs, liver with grilled onions, and a daily special, which for that day was roast beef and boiled potatoes. With each of these dinner selections there was offered a selection of green beans, corn or coleslaw, and a bowl of the soup of the day, which for that Tuesday was celery.

His mouth watered while reading this promissory note of culinary delight. He was further enthused to see a waitress serve a customer a basket of rolls with butter while offering free-flowing refills of coffee. This left him unable to resist the impulse to go in.

After entering, though, he was immediately confronted with the reality that there was no hostess to discreetly take him to a booth. He could see just a fellow making change for a customer at a counter. That was in the opposing corner of the room by the street entrance.

The situation made Horace feel out of place. He was about to turn and leave when a woman's voice called out, "Need a seat, mister? We've got one free here at the counter!"

He replied awkwardly, "I… I hoped to get a booth!"

"A booth? No, I'm sorry, not at this time of day. Booths and tables are for groups, but we've got a nice seat right over here."

He looked at where she was pointing, and despite it being near the entry to the kitchen, the spot had a certain appeal. It was the lone seat where the counter turned and was separated from the rest of it by the gate to the kitchen.

So he replied, "Alright, I see it."

"Good, can I get you some coffee?"

"Yes, that would be fine, thank you!"

This was the start of a long stretch of lunch breaks that Horace would spend at Sally's Diner. He remembered with amusement how he grew comfortable sitting at that counter seat and was disappointed when it wasn't available. It gave him an unblocked view of the waitress who would one day become his wife.

It was anything but obvious that this could ever happen from the way things between them had started out. In addition to the broad chasm that separated their worlds financially, Horace had a blundering way of widening the gap further.

One night he worked later than usual and decided to take a meal at the diner before going home. There was a decent filling of the place, but the hectic aura of lunchtime with the clanging of dishes and the calls from waitresses to those cooking was now much more subdued.

He was delighted to find Kathleen still working and had a look on him that was uncommon as he was smiling brightly. She soon recognized him and said, "You can get a booth if you want. Things are slower at this time."

He thanked her, but added, "No, my usual spot will be fine!"

With that she returned the smile and said, "I know what you mean! The stools have more cushion than the other seats. I prefer them myself!"

He was tempted to reply that he liked the company there better but held it back. It would have been too forward on his part. The fact was that he was attracted to her but was thoroughly confused as to how he should show it. She had such a wonderful warm manner dealing with everyone in the place—

not only the customers. He just had to find some way of crossing the waitress–customer threshold.

Horace could tell that the other waitresses and the cooks that normally bantered back and forth with one another in abrupt tones had a much friendlier relationship with Kathleen. After discovering that she owned the business, he had at first concluded that this was the reason for the different treatment. He decided afterward though that it wasn't the case. She was in fact a wonderful and warm personality that everyone seemed to be drawn to, employees and customers alike.

Kathleen's happy personality was no accident. She worked at it. Horace had come to know one of her motivations a few months earlier. The opening came when he focused on an old lithograph that was mounted in a frame and hanging high on the wall behind the counter. Underneath it was painted quite skillfully, *"The happiness he gives is quite as great as if it cost a fortune."*

He asked Kathleen what this referred to and she replied, "Oh, that's a picture of Fezziwig's shop as he and the boys were getting things ready for their Christmas celebration."

"Oh, I never heard of the fellow! What did he do?"

"Sure you have! Remember the book 'A Christmas Carol' by Dickens? Everyone's heard of that. Why, I can't remember a Christmas season that I missed returning to it!"

Horace was a little embarrassed but stated honestly, "No, I'm sorry, but you have that one on me. I never read it. I admit that I've heard of a movie by that name but haven't had the opportunity or the desire to see it. Christmas is just another day of the year to me. My mother..." Then his voice just trailed off as he caught himself.

To that Kathleen stated emphatically, "My Goodness man, that is surely a pity! I just can't imagine it! You've missed so much, and I can't take the time right now to fill the void. I'll tell you this though-old Fezziwig had a great gift. His was a grand exuberance for life, and it spread about onto all of those that came close to him. The fellow lived his life like the bright white snows that blanket the harshness of our city.

"My mother, the fine courageous woman that she was, taught me about him a long time ago. It was, in fact, just before she died of the cancer. She stated in no uncertain terms that I would always be successful with my life here if I ran this diner with the same love, compassion, and enthusiasm that Mr. Fezziwig did his business.

"That was a very difficult time for me, but the fact that I'm still here is a testament to the truth of her words. Whenever I am tempted to feel sorry for myself or curse misfortune or having to deal with a customer being rude, I look up at old Fezziwig, and he gets me through it.

"Let me tell you something. If you care about who you are, just one little bit, you would get a copy of that book right now and read it from cover to cover! You know, I can do one even better! Go out the front door to that little antique shop right across the street and tell Frank that I sent you. I happen to know that he has a couple of used copies of the book on a shelf!"

Do you know that Horace was so caught up in a trance with Kathleen that he marched right out and did exactly as she had told him? The next day he let her know as much, and she commented with an air of satisfaction, "Well, that's good! I'm happy for you. I hope it worked a little of its magic."

He couldn't help but reply with a smile, "Yes, I can tell you that it definitely has!"

Unfortunately, he saw the book as just a means to get closer to this lovely woman that attracted him so greatly. Scrooge reminded him of his mother and grandfather. By this point of his life he had managed to distance himself from both of them. His good grandmother had died, making the process of separation easy for him.

No, he didn't want to read about Scrooge any more than he would want to spend the holiday with his mother. If, however, he had taken some time to absorb how the carol's deep lessons related to his own decisions, he might have prevented a ghost from visiting him. It was one that had suddenly come from his past and was now lurking quite close.

Let us return though to Horace's recollection of that particular nighttime visit to the diner. After the room thinned out a bit, he saw Kathleen walking about the room assisting a little old woman. The lady was wrapped in a shawl and wearing clothes that looked worn and dated. They stopped by select tables and booths and made some conversation with the patrons at each.

He was curious at this and when they were walking back to the counter, his eyes followed their movement. Kathleen caught his watching them and seemed to question herself for a moment. Finally she approached Horace with the lady as she had the other customers.

When they reached him, Kathleen said, "Sir, you have been in here regularly, and I wondered if you would like to partake in a little ritual that we do with Mrs. McGinney here."

Horace had no clue as to what she had in mind and replied, "Well, what is the nature of this business?"

Kathleen was caught off-guard with his choice of words and answered, "Business, no, this is not business! I'm sorry, I was wrong to approach you."

She started to turn away, with her arm around the lady's shoulders. He felt from her response that he had done something to displease her and called out, "Honestly, ma'am, I didn't know your intention! What is it you want me to do?"

Kathleen looked back and replied softly, "This is not something for you to do because I want it. It must come from your heart."

"Well, I can't do what I don't understand. Can you help me?"

She called back, "Just a minute!"

Kathleen brought the women over to a booth and assisted her to sit down. After which she called out toward the kitchen, "Joe, can you bring that plate out now, please?"

In a second a fellow came out from the kitchen with a tray. He went across the room and set about serving a meal to the old woman. In the meanwhile, Kathleen waited on some other customers.

Horace realized that the man that Kathleen called Joe had remained standing by the woman the whole time she was eating, always ready to assist her. He even wiped her mouth when she was finished. Horace recognized this guy then as the same fellow that took money at the front of the restaurant at lunchtime. When the woman was finished, Joe sat opposite her in the booth and talked with her, but they were too far away for Horace to hear what they were saying.

Kathleen finally came back and sat at a stool at the counter just to the other side of the kitchen gate. She carefully set down a cup of steaming coffee, leaned her head down while raising the cup to take a little sip. After which she blurted out, "Ahh... I couldn't live without this stuff!"

She then casually looked over to Horace and said, "I'm sorry, Mack. I made a guess but was wrong. Sometimes customers like to partake in our little scheme to help Mrs. McGinney. You obviously don't know about her. I thought for a moment when you were staring at us that you did."

"Well, how about if you fill me in?"

"Actually, it's too long of a story for a stranger to grasp in one sitting. Most customers that know it have heard parts here and from others who have businesses around the area, like Ben, Frank, Vito, and Mrs. Dunn. The short version though is that Mrs. McGinney is an angel of sorts. She spent a lifetime helping those that needed it. Now that she is the one that is needy, we see it as an opportunity to repay her a little."

Horace couldn't help it, but the whole concept of giving aid to others was foreign to him. He had a lifetime of cold experiences and these masked the few little joyful ones. Nowhere in his past could be found an eye-opening story that would change his narrow view. There were no inspirational books or movies that influenced him like "A Christmas Carol" or "It's A Wonderful Life." Most importantly there was no recounting of Jesus Christ the Savior coming into our world as a little baby and living a life of the most exquisite example of giving to the human race. Horace's mother had no use for religion. No, all of this was treated by her as the old and selfish Mr. Potter had proclaimed, "Sentimental hogwash!"

Still, despite all of this, there was one thing that Horace was sure he didn't want to do and that was lose his access to Kathleen. He even loved her name since the first time he saw it on the little badge that was attached to her uniform. It sounded like a part of a song to him. Kathleen, Kathleen, Kathleen. When alone he spoke it out loud a hundred different ways and was not satisfied that he had exhausted the possibilities.

His mind went 'round and 'round in a frantic whirl. He had not only messed up an opportunity to grow closer to her, he had likely done just the opposite of growing closer. How could he find the key to repairing things? What could possibly be a way to have her return to the moment she had considered him for something that she felt was so important?

Finally, for the lack of anything else he could consider, he offered the one thing that he understood oh-so very well by stating, "Money? Is that what she needs? I have money!"

Kathleen looked over at him suddenly with a stunned look. She jumped up, lunged toward him, and placed her hand over his mouth all in one continuous motion. Finally, after an awkward period of maintaining that posture and regaining her composure, she said quietly, "You don't have a clue yet, do you?

He started to mumble something, and she held her hand tighter and added, "No, I'm sorry! I didn't mean for that to come out as a question! Don't say anything. Promise me! Just nod your head, and I will take my hand down."

So he did.

After a moment of thinking, she said to him in a very low voice, almost a whisper, "Look fella, it's obvious to me that you just don't understand. I was hesitant to tell you what I did for a reason. It's my fault, and I can only hope that she didn't hear you. I feel obligated now though to explain it to you further. If for no other reason, I'm doing this to keep you from making such an inappropriate outburst again!"

He just looked at her dejectedly like a naughty puppy being scolded. She paused for a moment and after taking a deep breath continued with, "The one thing that Mrs. McGinney still has is a little dignity. It hasn't always been that way. For years and years every extra penny that she and her husband toiled for was used to help other people. When her husband died though, it was like the sky fell in on her. The bank foreclosed, and they took away her home. She had - at eighty years old - already outlived everyone she was related to, even her two children. The poor lady was ignorant of the law and for the next five years failed to even collect the social security due to her.

"Yet with all her suffering she never let on to anyone how bad things were. From the little she made as a cleaning lady she couldn't even afford to live in a small apartment. Instead she would get a bed each night at the shelter to the southeast of here on Halsted Street.

"We finally were made aware of her condition one day when she slipped and fell, and Ben offered to take her home. That was when we found out where she was sleeping. Ben and Frank proceeded to find a nursing home that would take her in. We went to visit her there each week, and she would always say, "I wish I could return to the streets and help the needy people." She never once thought about herself.

"This led us to agree that we would take turns granting her wish. Once per month we pick her up from the home so she can visit the street where she had helped so many others in the past. She doesn't know about the money we collect for her. We tell her it's from a bank account that she had put money into in the past. The truth is that she gave all her money away a long time ago. She thought it was gone, but we keep telling her it is the interest that she continues to earn.

"Now she spends all of her time finding people that she feels are needy. Some of them are from the families of other folks at the nursing home. It's quite remarkable to see the effect on the people being helped. They would never have imagined in their wildest dreams that a little old woman from a nursing home would be coming to their aid. We have heard over and over of folks coming to visit their relatives in the home in an effort to give thanks. People got curious and wanted to see what had lifted the spirits of their mothers and fathers, grandmothers and grandfathers. For some of them it had been a long, long time.

"When Mrs. McGinney comes here we walk her around, and she asks our patrons if they know of anyone needing help. Afterward, those who can, contribute without her knowing. We show her the money, and she tells us where to send it. Every time we do this, she lights up when we say that there's still some money left in her account."

Horace thought about this for a moment and stated, "I'm not really sure about all of this. I've always been taught that the best way to help someone make money is to become their competition. If they're any good at it, they will rise to the challenge. It's not natural for me to feel sorry for someone that frittered their money away with no consideration for their own future. People need to take care of themselves first, don't they? It's only common sense!"

"Frittered away? You're sincere in this, aren't you? You just don't get it!"

She thought for a second and said, "That's too bad. You're not a bad-looking guy. What a bag of tricks though. It would probably take a lifetime to straighten you out!"

That's when Horace replied from his heart instead of from logic for the first time since he was a child, "Well, it would be a life worthwhile if you were the one doing it!"

She gave him a surprised look and after a short pause said, "Well, if I thought there was a heart in there some place, I might take a shot at it!"

That comment caught him speechless!

She thought about all of this for a second and then added in a low voice, "So you rate everything in terms of money, do you? Well, take out your wallet!"

He looked at her, bewildered, but did what she asked and reached over to set it on the counter in front of her. She picked it up and after seeing some large bills inside it, her eyes widened. She reacted with, "Holy crap, there must be a thousand dollars in here!"

Kathleen stared at him intently. It was obvious that she was having second thoughts. She finally shed those though and pulled all of the money out.

This certainly got Horace's attention, but he worked very hard to hide it.

She asked him, "What's your name?

He told her and she added, "Ok, Horace, I figure that I should at least know the name of someone I'm stiffing for such a large wad of the green!"

Horace remained quiet while taking it all in.

She turned her head and called out, "Hey, Joe, come over here for a minute, would you?"

Joe pardoned himself from Mrs. McGinney and walked over. Kathleen, in a continued low voice, said to him, "Joe, this high-crust guy named Horace here has heard about Mrs. McGinney. He was so moved by her kindness that he wants to contribute to the fund!"

Joe's face lit up, and he happily replied, "Hey, that's great! I'm sure that she will be delighted to hear that she earned more interest just in time for the holidays!"

Kathleen handed him the wad, and Joe just stared at it for a moment in amazement. All he could mutter while taking it was, "Wow, some interest!"

After that Kathleen walked over to Mrs. McGinney with Joe and said her goodbyes. Joe helped the old woman with her coat, pulled on his own, and the two of them left the restaurant. Kathleen then walked back by Horace and stated simply, "Well, we'll be closing now!"

Horace stared back at her, determined not to flinch. It was like she was calling his bluff in a high-stakes game of poker. Suddenly something occurred to him. His face flushed, and he was prompted to state to her meekly, "Would you mind lending me some change for the train? That was everything I had!"

She just looked at him for an extended moment coyly and then finally said, "I don't know about giving money to someone that hasn't looked out for his own future!"

Hearing this, all that Horace could do was smile. She smiled back and asked, "Well, Horace, where are you headed?"

"I've got an apartment in Lincoln Park."

"Fine then, it's your lucky day. I just happen to be going in that direction!"

Six months later the two were married in a little church ceremony. Joe and one of the restaurant waitresses were their witnesses. Otherwise, just her friends attended.

Horace soon discovered that more than anything else in the world, Kathleen's dream was to settle down and have a family. As reluctant as he was to deal with the responsibility of having a child, there was nothing that he would have refused her. A year later they had a daughter and named her Caroline.

Kathleen became a stay-at-home mom after selling the restaurant to Joe. In a few years he sold out too. Despite a couple of tries by others, none were able to make a success of the business as Kathleen and her mother had done.

Despite Horace's deep love for Kathleen, he continued to be blocked from being demonstrative with his feelings. He blamed this on his mother. Kathleen constantly prodded him to just let those bad feelings go. She also worked hard to help him achieve some spiritual enlightenment and to satisfy her he started to attend church services. It seemed to her that he was making some headway when his mother passed away.

Just before that he had gone to see her in the hospital. She had hardly a fraction of the presence she used to command. Her form was shrunken, her eyes were sunk-in, and her hair was white and unkempt. It was such a contrast to the black-haired, steely-eyed woman that she had been.

Horace thought for the first time, "She actually would have been seen as quite a beautiful woman in her younger years, if her cold and hard personality hadn't blocked it!"

He stood before her as she sat in a wheelchair. It was quite an effort for him to force out the words but somehow he managed, "Mother, this is Horace."

She didn't react. Her illness was consuming and her eyes just stared ahead. Horace tried one more time, louder, "Mother, this is Horace, your son. Can you hear me?"

Just that moment he was shaken to the core because her arms shot up and her hands grasped his wrists in a vise hold! Her eyes lifted slowly to his, and she stared with an intense look that further unnerved him. She then opened her mouth, but in what seemed to him an eternity of waiting, she didn't utter a sound.

Finally a nurse came and removed her hands from him. Her mouth closed, her eyes fell, and she took on the same spaced-out look that she had worn earlier. The nurse told him in a considerate tone, "She needs to rest now. She can't exert herself; it's too taxing."

The nurse was right, because his mother passed away that very night.

When he got home he discussed the visit with Kathleen. He was perplexed by why his mother had grabbed hold of his arms. He could only assume that it was her last effort in life to control him. This thought devastated Horace, and he wondered with anguish, "If she knew how I felt, like a kind of Frankenstein that has now outlived its creator, would that please her? Was it not enough that I was the image of her coldness for her own lifetime? Why couldn't she just let me be?"

It was obvious that the man was despondent, and Kathleen did her best to console him. She said that maybe his mother was in fact reaching out for forgiveness. This was something, though, that he just couldn't accept. There was no precedent for it in a life of experiencing her coldness.

CHAPTER SIX

The Secret

Matt suddenly called over to Horace, startling him out of his thoughts, "How about finishing my other hand? Seems like the baby's all right now."

Horace answered, "Fine, I'll get to it in a second."

First he walked over to the shop door and opened it for a second. He saw that it was still a nightmare of blowing snow with the wind whirling the stuff about in every way imaginable. He quickly shut it against a blast while exclaiming, "It's really awful out there. I hope Stash finds his wife!"

Then he walked to Matt and set about working with the glass fragments again, this time on his right hand.

He asked Matt, "Are you right handed?"

Matt replied that he was.

Horace added, "I guess we should have asked you earlier. If we had done your right hand first, you could have used it to help yourself!"

"That's what you would have preferred, isn't it? I figure that it must gall you to be helping me!"

Horace stopped suddenly with a stunned look and stared at him. In a moment he found some words and replied, "Look, Mr. Miller, we got off to a bad start earlier, but there's no reason to go on with these hard feelings. We're strangers, and when Stash comes back for his baby and the weather lets up we can return to our different worlds and pretend we've never met one another. The least you could be is a little civil. I helped you with your one hand, didn't I? It shouldn't take long, and I'll be done with the other. After all, it wasn't me that put the glass in your hands!"

To this Matt made no comment. He just clenched his teeth and closed his eyes as Horace continued to remove the pieces that were imbedded the deepest. After several minutes of this, however, Matt assessed that the bulk of the job had been done and said to Horace, "Stop for a second!"

Horace did, and Matt worked his fingers to close and open several times. Horace assumed the hand had been falling asleep, but Matt had other motives. He got a cynical smile and as some devious thoughts passed through his mind he said, "Go ahead!"

With that, Horace continued with the tedious process of picking at the smaller particles. As this went on, Matt couldn't hold back his angst and suddenly he blurted out, "So you really don't remember me, do you? Well, isn't that just like you!"

Horace stared at him again with disbelief and replied, "I admit that when I heard your name it sounded somewhat familiar. Try as I did though, I couldn't place you. I assumed you were someone in my building after seeing you in the lobby today but that's the length of it!"

Matt considered this and added, "That's so very convenient, isn't it? You live on your own little isolated island, don't you? Why would you bother to remember someone that you totally destroyed? How wonderfully convenient that is for you!"

Horace was really taken aback by this and retorted, "Of all the nerve! You miserable cretin! You let me help you by removing glass from your hands that got there as a result of your own stupidity and then you have the gall to accuse me of wronging you! You're out of your mind!"

"Your helping me, ah yes, that was the beauty of it. It set the stage for such sweet revenge! Fate got in the way for a little while, but now there is nothing to stop me!"

Horace stared back at him and started to sweat. He backed away a step and asked, "Revenge, what do you mean, revenge?"

"Ah yes, Mr. Stone and Steel, I've finally permeated that tough exterior haven't I? You want to know what kind of revenge? Well, I mean to show you!"

With that he reached in behind his suit coat lapel and dug for something underneath. Suddenly he pulled out a small gun and pointed it directly at Horace. Terrified at the sight of it, Horace backed away several more steps.

After a short silence, Matt said in a low and vicious tone, "Don't worry now, Horace! I'm not going to shoot...yet! I think we should have a little trial here first, before I give you your sentence!"

Horace tried hard to form some words, but could only eke out, "Trial, what sort of trial?"

"Well, we want to be civilized here, don't we? A man shouldn't receive his punishment without being reminded of his crime. No, Horace, I can't let you off that easy! You're going to hear all the sordid little details. Then I'm going to kill you!"

Horace replied in as convincing a tone as he could muster, "I'm not afraid of dying. Say what you will. I've done nothing to you!"

Inside his head, though, he fought with the idea that anyone would hate him so! He wondered, "What could I possibly have done to this man for things to come to this? There's nothing I know of! He's just lost it totally. He's out of his mind!"

He then considered as a desperate measure, "I have to try to humor him, if not for my own sake, for that of this little baby!"

Just as if the baby had been able to take in the threat, it started to fuss. This caught Matt off guard and he blurted out, "Let it cry! A little crying never hurt any baby!"

Horace responded, "Stash said that if it cries it's hungry or needs to be changed!"

"I don't give a damn what Stash said, it doesn't need anything right this second!"

Horace waited a moment as the baby's cry escalated. He stated softly, "Whatever grudge you hold for me, this baby is an innocent. Can't you remember how Stash, his father, came to your aid? Let me see what the baby needs and then you can proceed as you want."

"You're not determining anything, you hear?"

To this Horace said nothing, but his mind churned further with how he might in fact change things. Finally, Matt added, "Yeah, Stash. He's lucky that he didn't get shot! I said he was touching my billfold, but the fact was that he got a little too close to my equalizer here!"

"Is that your idea of justice? Shoot some fellow while he's trying to help you?"

"Don't you lecture me! I wouldn't have shot him! Unless that is he tried to stop me! I've been waiting too long for this opportunity. I waited and planned and I will wait no more!"

Horace cringed as he thought Matt had decided to shoot. Instead though he was getting irritated by the baby's continued crying and yelled to him, "Do something about that screaming kid right now!"

Horace moved over slowly by the baby and said, "I have to open the baby bag and get out his diapers and bottle."

Matt called out abruptly in a commanding tone, "Wait...I'll do it!"

After which he walked from behind the table and fumbled a bit to open the zipper of the baby bag with his free hand. He finally turned it over and shook out the contents. Seeing what was there, he backed away while stating, "Alright, go ahead!"

Horace followed the natural instinct of trying to feed the baby first. He held the nipple of the bottle by the baby's lips and hoped that the formula was what he wanted. Considering how things might develop though, he thought he should shift attention away from the baby. He didn't know how far Matt would go if he continued to be irritated by its crying. Fortunately the child opened its little mouth and latched onto the nipple like a baby goat.

He thought, "He's sucking on it like he hasn't eaten in days!"

Matt interrupted the silence with, "No sense wasting time now, is there? Did you think you were getting a little break, a kind of stay of execution? Well, dream on! No, you can just listen to the evidence while you're pacifying the kid."

There was a moment of quiet and Matt added, "The first point against the accused is that he is a pompous ass!"

Horace stared over at him with disdain, but Matt continued undeterred with, "Yes, there he is, Horace Williams, the great performer. Salesman supreme! Deal maker, home breaker! Yes, you were the king, weren't you? You could do no wrong as far as all the great powerbrokers were concerned.

"You must have loved how all the other salesmen bowed to your accomplishments. Try as they might, they couldn't even come close to your level. You were their god. Everyone wanted to touch the cloth of your thousand-dollar suits."

He stopped for emphasis and added, "Every man can be bested though. I was the one who had figured out how to do just that. I didn't hate you then. In fact, I too, emulated your success. I worked and schemed and contacted clients and flew countless hours to put together a deal bigger than even the great Horace Williams could imagine. You somehow found out though, didn't you? Try as you might you couldn't beat me, so you set about destroying me!"

Horace had had enough of this and shot back, "I did nothing of the sort, but now I remember who you were. I didn't know you, but I knew of you. It's true; you were becoming a force to be reckoned with. My boss said that you were a great player. I heard your name bantered about by other staff too. But I never had a thing to do with you! All I heard was that you just evaporated. It was the common belief that you left to start your own business. Everyone waited for you to suddenly emerge in the industry and become a major player."

Matt took this in and responded with, "I expected you to run for cover with your life on the line. You needed no cover then, did you? You were protected. You were like gold, preserved for eternity. You had the contract that was iron clad. No one, not even the people that purchased the company could touch you. You made sure that the law was on your side, and you are still riding on that magic carpet, aren't you? At least, that is, until tonight. Your contract can't protect you from this!"

While Horace stood in disbelief of what he was hearing he had unconsciously pulled the bottle away from the baby's mouth. Again he started to fuss. Matt took this in and added, "Losing your touch? Can't do two things at the same time? You could manage it quite easily then, though, couldn't you?"

Horace adjusted position and after seeing the baby was again satisfied, replied, "The way I understand it now, you are blaming me for your failing to make a deal. How was it that I did that?"

"Playing cagey, are we? Buying time, is that what your scheme is? I bet you are hoping that someone else will come in here. Well if they do, you can count on one thing. I'll get you first."

Horace thought for a second and retorted, "To the contrary, I have no hope that someone else will come in here and risk their lives. As it is, you are doing this with no concern for this baby. If you kill me, are you just going to run out and leave him here? You can't leave an infant by himself!"

"I don't intend to leave, you old fool! Once I kill you, my purpose for living is over. They can do what they want with me. I have nothing else thanks to you!"

This statement made Horace reach deep for answers. He couldn't help but blurt out, "Your whole life was based on one deal? How is that possible?"

"That's the view you take now, isn't it, when you've already reached the top. Well I hadn't! I had scraped together and spent every facet of my existence on that deal! I mortgaged my home to the limit, borrowed from relatives—even the ones that repulsed me.

"I needed money, a lot of money, to put the scheme together. Traveling, wining, and dining every possible suit that could make the difference. I had it in my hand. I could feel it! I could taste it! I was never so certain of anything, ever! But you found a way to steal that sale away and bury it where it was of no use to anyone. All it took was one lousy signature. A few strokes of a pen...and I was finished!"

Horace broke in with, "You say I signed something? You are mad! What could I sign to make you lose your deal?"

"Enough of this crap! You ran sales, and they moved you up. Everyone knew of your contract! You made them pay the price!"

Horace thought, "That damned contract. Will it ever stop giving me grief?"

He fell into a reliving of that morning. Kathleen had stopped him before leaving their home and said, "Horace, listen now, I've made a decision. I'm going to leave today. You won't come with me, so I'm just going myself. I can't live without Caroline, Tom, and the children. I'm leaving! When you come home I won't be here. You will have to fend for yourself!"

This really shocked Horace, to the point his hands started to shake. He stared at her and replied, "You're leaving me! Just like that with no warning! How can you do that?"

"Horace, don't put it that way! We've discussed this. You refuse to leave the city because of that wretched contract! You made your choice. I tried to convince you for so long that the money is not important. We are losing something so much more valuable. I won't spend another Christmas without seeing our Caroline and her family. I'm going to act like a grandparent now, with or without you!"

Horace couldn't help himself. He was locked on the words, "I'm leaving!"

His heart was beating wildly! He felt it ringing in his ears and blurted out, "You're divorcing me? Is that what this is? Someone has to tell me. I must know the truth!"

In his mind he was a child again, standing up in the courtroom, yelling out this time, "Is this a divorce? Father, are you leaving me? Please look at me, father! Why won't you look at me?"

A voice finally penetrated the vision. He heard a low repetition of, "Horace, Horace, Horace, please listen to me!"

Finally he saw Kathleen's face as she was exclaiming, "I'm not divorcing you, Horace! Why can't you understand? I'm so worried about you now! Did you take your pill? The doctor said you can't miss it! Do you understand me? I am not divorcing you!"

As his hearing and vision finally cleared, he replied, "Alright, I do, I hear you! You are not divorcing me. All right then, I have to get some air. I'll call you tonight. I'll call you at Caroline's. I'll call you. Everything's fine now. I took my pill. Yes, I understand!"

"Oh, Horace, I hate to see you this way! We'll talk about this later. Here, take your pills with you! If you feel weak, you need to take another one, remember!"

He took the bottle in his hand and deposited it into his coat pocket while saying, "I understand! I have to leave now, or I'll be late."

So he did leave, but the incident haunted him all day. He thought nothing could have been worse. Now he realized he was wrong. This man was intent on divorcing him from his family forever!

He focused on Matt who was staring at him, who said to Horace mockingly, "Back from Never-Never Land? You can't hide from the truth now, can you?"

"You mentioned my contract. I found that to be a prison instead of a grand achievement. Yes, I go on with the company, but they have the power, not me. I ensured I would be given continued employment, and they had it interpreted literally. I didn't stipulate when I could take vacation time, and

I wanted the option to work between the holidays even if everyone else took off. They got a court to interpret that as my never being off between or in the month of major holidays. I was a fool!"

He stopped for a moment to get his breath and then added, "If I ever do take off, the contract is voided, and they can terminate me! It would mean the loss of a great sum of money. Money I intend to give to my daughter and her family. The price I pay is never being able to see my daughter and family during the holidays because they live in California. Now my wife has left me to be with them. Is that something to envy?"

The baby was fussing again, and Matt exclaimed, "Give him the bottle, damn it!"

"The milk is gone!"

"Well, change him then!"

"Yes, yes, it'll take a minute!

As he did though, he added, "I wish that I could talk to Kathleen now. I would go with her. If I had, I wouldn't be here - to hell with that money! That's where it belongs!"

"You old fool! You dare to make yourself a martyr after what you did to me. Do you think you are the only one in the world that has lost their family? I had a wife, I had kids. I had four of them! But they're all gone now!"

As Horace fumbled with removing the baby's diaper, Matt went into a trance of his own. He suddenly continued with, "Marge just couldn't understand what we lost! She told me to start again and to just forget it! Well I started again alright, but I couldn't forget. I wouldn't forget! You don't forget someone that has done something so awful to you."

Again after lingering, he added, "I tried. I tried, but fate just wouldn't let me. Why did the only job that was available to me appear in the same building of the man that I held so much contempt for? Marge told me, don't take it, but I was determined to overcome all that you were.

"Try as I did, you had to just keep popping up, in the elevator, on the street, even sometimes when I sought solitude at the library! It ate at me that you could look indifferent when we passed. I was just a bump in your road.

"I tried everything. I saw psychologists, I attended programs, I even talked to a priest, but there was no getting you out of my head. Finally Marge wouldn't listen anymore. I knew that she was no longer on my side. She insisted that I leave. You talk about not spending holidays with your family! Well, you took care of that for me too, didn't you? I can't see them now or ever!"

Horace had stopped changing the baby when Matt was saying this. As it lay there naked, he stared at Matt and replied, "I don't know how I did it, but if I made you lose your family, I am truly sorry. I can't imagine anything that would be worse!"

"It's too late! Don't say it! It's too late to be sorry! What does that give me back? Nothing, that's what, nothing!"

Horace was feeling dizzy. Matt's figure was drifting in and out of focus. He tried to steady himself by leaning against the table the baby was on.

Matt started again with, "So now I'll continue with the evidence. There is just one more thing, but I have saved the best for last!"

He tried to reach into his other suit-jacket pocket with his free hand, but it was too awkward for him to reach. The handkerchief bandage pulled away partially, and it must have caught on a sliver still imbedded because he groaned. He worked the bandage back in place with the gun hand and switched the gun to the other. Finally he found what he had been looking for. It was a sheet of common copy paper folded over twice.

With some added effort he managed to unfold it. He approached the table where the baby was lying and set the paper next to him. While standing back with the gun again, he pointed it at Horace and stated, "There it is, the proof that seals the coffin. That's all that is needed. I managed through a great effort to get it. You had no idea, but I slipped into your office. It must have been right after they gave you your grand reward. You were right at the top with control to move mountains. Yes, you moved one then and dumped it on me!"

Horace replied, "Office, on top, I don't know what you are talking about!"

"You will deny it even now? That tact won't work with me! You want to hear the details? Yes, I'll give you details. You couldn't let me steal your thunder, could you? I was bringing in a great deal, three times the size of the largest one you ever had. That made it bigger than the one that elevated you to be a partner.

"When you discovered my scheme, you couldn't accept it. They might reconsider your position. They might think I should be the one up there in the clouds! So you convinced them to sell. You went to the company I was dealing with, and you talked them into buying ours out. If they owned the firm, they wouldn't need my deal! They wouldn't need the one that had bested you! You are a conniving son of a bitch, and you're going to pay now for what you did to me!"

With that he demanded, "Look at the paper! Look at the proof."

Horace picked the paper up with his shaking hands. After reading it, he just shook his head and stated, "I can't believe that this piece of paper has been the focus of so much grief for you and your family. God help you!"

"That's all you can say with the proof lying there in front of you? 'God help me!' No, I already tried that route. You, say your prayers old man!"

Horace did just that and a thought came to him and he stated, "Could I ask for a few more seconds, surely that can't make a difference?"

Matt replied suspiciously, "You're stalling. A few seconds for what?"

"I want to just give you something from my wallet."

Matt stared at him in disbelief and replied, "You fool! Do you think you can bribe me? No amount of money in the world could stop me now!"

"No, I am not bribing you! I'm trying to enlighten you and perhaps in the process help you to save your soul."

"Save my soul! That takes a lot of nerve for someone like you to say! Save my soul? Who is going to save yours?"

"I'm trying to do that too."

"I don't care about your soul, old man!"

Horace thought for a moment and said, "Look, Matt, you have stated your case and have provided your evidence. I read it as you told me. Now I'm just asking that you read something that is in my wallet."

Matt was wild with the frustration of prolonging things and looked to the door of the shop and quickly back to Horace. He finally stated, "You have twenty seconds. I've waited long enough!"

Horace fought his hand into his pocket and that little effort made him start to feel dizzy again. After just managing to pull out his wallet, he had to lean against the table again to steady himself and tried to hold it open. He was relieved to find the card. While emitting a groan, he leaned across the table and dropped the card with his wallet onto the table. Try as he might though he couldn't push himself back up. His arms were held out stiff to just hold up his weight as the baby lay precariously below him.

He grunted, "Look at the card, please!"

Matt wondered whether Horace was just putting on an act or actually having some kind of attack. Horace made a quieter effort to speak again and said, "Look at the card!"

Something made Matt finally reach down and pick it up. He stared at it and after focusing could see that it was Horace's business card.

It read, *'Horace C. Williams.'*

Under that there was just, *'Sales Department.'*

Matt continued to stare at it while thinking and said, "What are you trying to tell me here, Horace, that you aren't a bigwig in the company anymore? Well, so what? You were when you ruined me! You were then!"

Something else occurred to him though. He looked hard at the card and picked up the sheet of paper. He stared at it and said, "No, that's not right! It's not possible!"

The signature on his sheet was clearly H. R. Williams.

He wondered, "Why doesn't it match? Did he change it somehow? Why would he have changed it?"

He started to doubt this and said, "No, it must be a typing error! Who else could it be?"

He spotted Horace's open wallet unfolded with his license displayed in a clear holder. He snatched it up and pulled it over by the sheet and compared the signature on the license with that on the letter.

No matter how carefully or how long he looked at them, no matter how much he closed and opened his eyes, when he refocused the two Williams' signatures just didn't look the same. He lost his breath and fell back against the counter bellowing, "No, no, this can't be!" How is this possible?"

The realization was setting in. If Horace was not the man responsible, who was? Try as he did, he just couldn't find another face to replace that of Horace's. It was just too hard to contemplate, too much to accept and this left him just staring ahead.

As Horace looked up he realized that the look in Matt's eyes was just like that of his mother on that last day he had seen her. It was a look of desperation by a man that now knew he was wrong. He wondered, "Was that what she was feeling? Was she reaching out to me in remorse? Was my dear Kathleen right? Oh my God!"

From deep down in Matt's soul a wisp of truth slipped through to his conscious mind, and his face contorted with the strain that it caused him. The truth became thoughts. They were punishing thoughts that revealed that he, not Horace, was the one that was wrong. Somehow in his drive for success it had blinded him. He had made his loss so large that it demanded that he find someone to blame. In his hurry to do that he looked past the one that did it and found the one instead that he had envied. Horace was the easy one to hate.

Now the man looked as innocent as the baby lying below him. He was near collapse from the ordeal that Matt had just put him through!

Matt looked inside himself for an answer, some escape from the walls that were closing in on him. Try as he did though, he couldn't find one. A thought finally came to mind, and his face relaxed as he slowly moved his gun hand up next to his head.

Just then, Horace slumped down on top of the baby. Matt heard a little muffled baby cry, but it abruptly stopped. He stared down at Horace, and his look of fear returned. The gun dropped with a smack against the floor. Matt lunged toward the table and with a groan, rolled Horace over and off the baby.

Little Johnny cried again for a second, and Matt stared down at his face. Looking up then, he just cooed and smiled. Matt gave in to his mental exhaustion and stumbled back to fall into the chair. While resting his head in his scared hands, he sobbed,

"What have I done? My God, what have I done?"

CHAPTER SEVEN

The Journey

While Stash battled the storm, his first goal was to return to the train station. In his mind it was the only logical place for Julie to go after leaving the antique shop. He considered further, "If that was her!"

He recycled some of the last-second information offered by Horace. Based on their having arrived earlier that day at Union Station, Stash should run into it if he found Monroe Street and went east for several blocks.

Unfortunately the storm was unrelenting and the blowing snow had coated the street signs. He decided to take a shot and turn where some of the buildings looked familiar. After continuing for about two more blocks he was happy to find a sign that he could read. He was so relieved to confirm that he was in fact on Monroe. This served to increase his determination, and he used every ounce of strength that he could muster to get closer to the station.

In that stretch it occurred to him that Julie would freak out when she saw that he didn't have their baby. He would have to explain convincingly that little Johnny was in good hands. He hoped upon hope that this was true! Everything depended on Horace following up on his promise.

Stash knew that the key to calming his wife was to quickly convince her that her assessment of the situation at the shop had been wrong. Horace and Matt came across as a little set in their ways but otherwise he thought they were harmless. He just couldn't take a chance on tramping about downtown Chicago carrying the baby in this awful storm. If Julie wasn't at Union Station, who could say where he might have to go to find her?

The fact was that at that very moment Julie stood in a phone booth at the station. She had called the police and reported her concerns about the men in her dad's shop. The man she talked to said that there had already been a call relating to that location and asked if she was the one that had made it. She replied that she wasn't and said again that her concern was for her father. With this new information, the dispatcher promised that they would get a car over there as soon as possible.

While waiting she wondered about who else would have called the police. It scared her to think that it could have been her dad, and she thought, "Maybe he locked himself in the back room when the men broke in!"

She considered this further with, "But there's no phone in there!"

Finally she rationalized, "He could have called from upfront before hiding in the back!"

All of this left Julie very frustrated and worried, and she wished there was some way to get hold of her dad. She had tried calling earlier that day on the possibility that he still had the old phone number from years before when she still worked there with him. That number, though, was disconnected, and none other was listed. She thought, "He probably has a cell phone or maybe he uses Ben's phone."

Suddenly that triggered, "Ben, yes, Ben, that's who I can try! Why didn't I think of that earlier?"

She dialed a number and sure enough it started to ring. There were several more that followed and she worried, "Oh

God, Ben's not there either. What was I thinking? It's Christmas Eve!"

But just that moment a soft voice answered with, "Hello hello!"

She exclaimed, "Ben, Ben, is that you?"

"Yes, this is Ben. Who is calling?"

"It's Julie, Ben...Frank's daughter, Julie. Remember me?"

"Julie...why of course I remember you, honey! I'm so glad, so relieved that you called!"

After a short pause he added, "Honey, I don't want to upset you, but I'm sitting here in the dark in my shop while worrying a blue streak about your daddy! Where are you? Did you speak to Frank? Do you know what's goin' on over in his shop?"

Realizing that they shared the same concerns, she told him what had happened to her. After which she added that she had called the police. Ben quickly confirmed that he was the one that had called them earlier. He breathed easier after hearing that the police would definitely be coming.

Julie thought to herself, "I should go there. That's where Stash was supposed to go with the baby. What if he's stuck in the shop now with the baby and those men? What about dad? Where is he?"

With all that in mind, she exclaimed to Ben, "I'm coming to your shop! I want to be there when the police arrive. I've got to find out where dad and my husband and baby are!"

"Your husband and baby? I didn't know you were married, Julie! Does Frank know?"

"No, dad doesn't know! I couldn't reach him! I planned earlier for us all to come today as a surprise! I was foolish I guess, but things are happening so fast that he just needs to know!"

Ben sensed the desperation in her voice and responded with, "Honey, I'm sure everything will be ok! When you come to my place, we can talk about it! It's dark in here though, because the power is out! I don't want you to be concerned with that! I'm fine. Just come in, and I'll be sitting right by the door."

Before leaving the station Julie asked a guard to keep a lookout for a man carrying a baby. She described his dress and stated that if his name was Stash, a note she provided was to be given to him.

As fate would have it, just as Julie exited through one set of doors, Stash came into the station through another.

Meanwhile, Ben sat thinking about how it had been a week of turmoil for him. He wondered and worried if he was at fault for whatever was happening to Frank. He had made a decision a few days before. It was based on his knowing that Frank had some serious health issues that he should be telling his daughter, Julie about. It had occurred to Ben that he might not be around that long himself. He wanted desperately for Frank and Julie to finally get together.

Years before, when Julie first started writing Frank letters, he received one and commented to Ben in an offhanded manner that he would just throw it away unopened. That's how bitter he had acted about her leaving. Ben though, insisted that Frank give the letters to him so that he could check that Julie was alright. Frank acted like he was conceding reluctantly, but a voice in his heart held out hope that she would come back.

Now in the present, there was a letter recently received in which Julie pleaded with Frank to call her. She stated further that there were some things that he needed to know, important things that she just couldn't trust to a letter. When Frank gave that one to Ben, he read it and knew that something really serious was going on. He tried to get Frank to look over it too, but as usual he was too stubborn and refused to hear a thing about it. For the first time this really upset Ben, and he called Frank an old fool.

Frank's reaction to Ben's words was to abruptly turn and leave the tobacco shop, and Ben hadn't seen him since. With that, he decided to wrap up all the letters from Julie that he had saved, and put them in a box. To it he attached a note. In it he wrote,

Dear Frank,

For years and years I have been reading letters from Julie while she tried desperately to stay in contact with you. I could never understand why you wouldn't read them. I must tell you, if there was any way that I could communicate with my son or Margelie, I would have done it immediately. But that option wasn't open to me. It's obvious now, based on Julie's last letter, that she really needs you.

If you can't help your own daughter, it means your heart light has gone out, and I can no longer be your friend. Please, Frank, read the letters! It might be your last chance with Julie. Fight away that stubbornness. It doesn't do anything that benefits you. Reach down inside and find a little compassion. I want to remain your friend. It's now up to you.

Ben

Now he was having second thoughts, starting with, "What if all of this tension and turmoil has been too much for Frank to deal with? He could have had a heart attack or something. Or maybe he was locked up in his back room hiding from the guys that broke in. Worse yet, they could have done something to him!"

He ached over this and considered, "If I didn't write that note, I think Frank would have come over here after he closed the shop as he has always done!"

Ben's mind drifted, and he thought again about Jesse, "Ah crap, I probably made a bad decision with him too. What's the matter with me lately?"

Jesse had been helping Ben with various tasks in his shop for over a year. The young man had actually gone into Frank's place first, looking for work. Frank sent him over to Ben, knowing that he needed the help more. Ever since Ben's eyes had started failing him, tasks around the shop had become a safety issue. He fell twice in a short period and in the latter case broke his hip. After the surgery he had to spend an extended period in rehab. It was the first time the shop was closed in twenty years!

To Ben, Jesse had been a godsend. The young man worked hard for him and proved to be honest. He also had a good business mind. Each day he would come in after taking a bus from his other employer that was located south of the Loop. Jesse would do anything that Ben asked. It was Jesse that had brought the package of Julie's letters and the note over to Frank's shop.

When he returned from the errand, Jesse said to Ben, "Mr. Simms, I have a business proposition for you. I talked with my mother, and she has been saving for years for me to go to college. I told her, 'Mama, I don't want to go to college! I have my own family now, and I want to have a shop like Mr. Simms and Mr. Fleming do. That is what I really want to do with my life!'

"Well, at first she didn't agree, but then she came around after I told her all the things I would do. So Mr. Simms, what I'm proposing is to buy your shop from you. Of course, you can continue to come here as long as you want. I know that being in here and visiting with your friend Frank across the street means a lot to you. So Mr. Simms, what do you think? Will you sell the place to me? If I don't have what you think the shop is worth, we can work something out! I can get a loan!"

This had really caught Ben off-guard. He had some big problems with the idea but knew if he turned Jesse down flat, that he would be crushed. That would probably make Jesse quit helping him. All he could think to do was say, "This is an important matter, Jesse, both for you and for me! I have to give it some serious thought. We will talk more about it after I do that."

"You're right, Mr. Simms, I understand! It's a big decision. I can wait for you to think about it. It's a pretty neat idea, though, don't you think?"

Ben tried hard to find the right words and all he could come up with was, "Well, it's certainly something for me to think about!"

Ben considered the subject further as he waited for Julie, "If Jesse does show up tonight, he will likely ask about buying the shop again."

The truth was that Ben held some serious reservations about the idea. It wasn't the money. If there were no other problems, he would just give it to him. He had no kin close by. Those he could remember lived in Detroit, and he had lost contact with them many years ago. Besides, he really liked Jesse. It was like he was given to him by God to replace his son.

The biggest problem he had with the shop was what he sold. It was one thing for him at seventy-five years old to sell all that tobacco stuff, but for Jesse, that was no way for him to commit his life.

Without the tobacco products though there was really nothing for Jesse to own. The shop space was leased and that contract would be up in two years. He knew the lease wouldn't be renewed. It had been originally made for fifty years by the original building owner who had befriended him and Frank. The man had used his clout to get the same deal for both of them after an incident where they played a key role in saving his life.

Their benefactor, though, was now long gone after retiring to a condominium in Florida. He had sold the building Ben was in, and the new owners could get five times the rent that he was paying per the lease. No, in two years there would be no more tobacco shop, because there would be no place to put it.

Unfortunately, he knew that Jesse would still want to buy it. The shop turned a profit. Ben didn't know how long the product would be saleable though. The city might decide soon to make tobacco sales illegal. They had already made moves to ban smoking in public places. He wondered, "What would Jesse do then?"

Ben felt down deep in his heart that the biggest problem for him selling the shop to Jesse was the moral one. Smoking tobacco killed people and in the process put them through a lot of hell. Fifty years before, it would have been hard to convince anyone of that, but now it was something you could bet on. No, this wasn't a business he would have given to his own son knowing these things, and he wouldn't give it to Jesse either. The possibility of losing Jesse as a friend, though, made Ben feel so sad. It would be like losing his son all over again.

Suddenly Ben was startled out of his thoughts by the shadow of someone looking through the door glass. He surmised that it was Julie or Jesse, so he got up to unlock it. A voice confirmed this with, "It's ok, Mr. Simms, it's only me, Jesse!"

"Jesse, I'm so glad you came!"

As he walked in, he tried the light switch by habit, and then exclaimed, "Oh wow, Mr. Simms, I see the power is out in here too! The street lights are all off, but I noticed that there's a light on in the bank across the street next to Frank's shop. That seems strange. Does Frank have power?"

"I don't know, Jesse, but I fear that losing power is the least of his problems."

Ben proceeded to bring Jesse up to speed on all of his concerns and what he thought he saw of the people coming and going from Frank's shop. He also explained about Julie, that she was on her way and had called the police.

Jesse commented, "That's cool Mr. Simms. They should be here soon. They'll take care of it, and Frank will be fine! I'm sure he will. You have had a lot of excitement and should try to relax!"

"I wish I was that sure, Jesse! I sure wish I was. If I could see better and this darned weather wasn't so terrible, I would go over there! I'm not afraid of facing bad guys. I did my share of that when I was in Korea. I just don't think I could get across the street with that darned wind gusting so hard!"

Jesse thought it would be best to just change the subject. He asked Ben, "Mr. Simms, you know I've been thinking a lot about the shop lately."

Ben thought, "Oh crap, here it comes!"

But Jesse continued with, "I started to wonder about how your dad came about having this place. Did his father give it to him?"

Ben felt like he had dodged a bullet. It wouldn't hurt telling him about his father. He didn't want to go too far back though, that might make him get even more attached to the idea of selling tobacco. He would instead just focus on his dad's time in Chicago and try to keep the story short. So he started with, "When my daddy came here, he was having some difficulty deciding how to proceed. He didn't have the same kind of connections that he had created down south. Back there he sold tobacco in its raw leaf condition, before it was processed into smoking or chewing products. The market up here worked differently. Everything was at a larger scale. Large sums of money were changing hands quickly.

"He held a decent sum of cash but wanted to make sure that he used it intelligently. That meant finding someone that could share their own experiences with the market mechanisms. One day he found such a man while talking over a drink at a local saloon. The gentleman's last name was Weatherbee."

"My dad said that Mr. Weatherbee came across to him as a decent fellow."

The man had instructed my dad in a sincere manner with, 'You should not play in this market unless you can walk away from a large loss without being crippled by it. Those trading here are used to very high stakes. It is true that fortunes can be made here but many have lost large for each one that wins. If you can't afford to lose, don't play the game!'"

"Dad understood well what the fellow was telling him. He could lose everything in one bad move. Such a risk wasn't even to be considered with his family depending on him. This left him wondering if he had made a grave error by bringing them all to Chicago. He left the tavern in a kind of bewildered condition after thanking Weatherbee for his advice.

"When he arrived back at the inn where his family was temporarily staying, he continued to be perplexed at what he might do to take care of them. He wasn't married yet so I wasn't even in the picture. He was however, looking, after his mother and siblings and a couple of other folk, including his future wife, that had worked with them on the plantation. Their needs were a heavy responsibility.

"By chance he again ran into Weatherbee on the following day. It was in this area we are in now. Dad was in the process of returning from a local bank where he had deposited his money, and Weatherbee was walking down the street with a book in hand. He continued to be friendly, so they stopped to discuss dad's dilemma in Sally's Diner. It was just next door. At that time her father ran the place, and it was more of a saloon than an eating establishment.

"For some reason, dad always emphasized a point when telling this story. The thing that struck him most with Weatherbee was the way the man hung on to that one same book all the time. Dad surmised that it must have been valuable to him for some reason. He guessed that it might have contained Weatherbee's notes for dealing in the market. I remember him mentioning in a reflection some years later that the man was involved in the trade of rare woods."

Ben suddenly broke off from this with, "I'm kind of getting off track here. Julie should be coming soon! Well, in any case, Weatherbee made a suggestion to dad. He thought that with what dad knew about tobacco that he should at least consider selling finished tobacco products like cigarettes, cigars, and the like.

"Well, dad took to that idea immediately. The first thing you know he was looking for a place to set himself up. By chance this place right here was available. He followed that by investigating suppliers of various products and in a short while managed to start a business. The rest is pretty much as I have already told you."

Ben deliberated further for a moment and then added, "Jesse, maybe you could help me! If we get over there and are careful we might be able to see what's going on."

"I don't think you should try that, Mr. Simms. The street is too slick for you to be walking on. We should wait for the police!"

"But who knows when they'll get here? With the storm and power being out, they might be too busy to come!"

Just as Jesse started to say, "Well, I co..."

There was another knock at the shop door, and Ben exclaimed, "That must be Julie!"

Jesse said, "I'll get it!"

He rushed over to open the door. Julie stood there covered with snow and said as she saw him, "Ben, where's Ben?

Jesse replied, "You must be Julie. Ben's right here!"

Hearing this, Ben spoke up, "I'm here, honey!"

She came in, and Ben stood up while saying, "I wish there was light! I could see you better!"

"Come here and give me a hug!"

She replied in a hesitant manner, "I'm full of snow, Ben, and I'm soaked from the sleet that blew through earlier!"

"Oh, a little snow and water won't kill me! Come here!"

She did, and they embraced. While that way, Julie exclaimed, "Oh, Ben, I'm so worried about my baby and Stash and dad. Where are they?"

"I'm worried too, honey! Hopefully the police will come soon. I'm turning into a nervous wreck!"

Just then, they heard the door open with a ring of the attached bell and just as quickly, it closed. Ben called out excitedly, "What was that?"

Julie ran to the door to look out while exclaiming, "Oh my Lord, your helper is running across the street!

"Oh no! Julie, please, his name is Jesse! Tell him I said to come back!"

She opened the door and tried calling, but he was already to the other side. With the wind howling, he wouldn't have heard her anyway.

Across the street then, after slowing his determined run, Jesse approached the shop with some caution. He then knelt down in some slush and tried to see through a little jagged piece of broken glass at the bottom of the door. There was a sliver of light emitted through it. He could only make out in the distance what looked like two legs standing.

All of a sudden he heard a voice cry out, "Oh my God, help me! I don't know what to do!"

Jesse jumped up, grasped the handle, and pushed the door open. With his view now illuminated he found himself staring at Matt.

The tormented man exclaimed, "Please! He needs help! I think he's dying!"

Just then Jesse spotted the gun lying on the floor and stopped suddenly while demanding, "Did you shoot him?"

"No, he's having a heart attack or something!"

Jesse looked all around the room and added, "Ok now, mister, don't you move!"

Jesse slowly advanced and suddenly reached down and grabbed the gun. With that in hand he demanded, "No funny business now! You move away from him and let me see!"

Matt did as he asked, and after inspecting the area Jesse exclaimed, "Holy shit, that's a baby! Whose baby is that?"

"A guy that's looking for his wife left him here."

"That must be Julie's baby!"

"Stash mentioned that name."

"But where's Frank? Did you do something with him? If you did I think I'd have to shoot you!"

"I don't know any Frank. The father's name was Stash."

There was a short lull as Jesse was sizing Matt up.

Matt asked with deep concern, "What about Horace here? He needs help! He's been out for a while now! I didn't know what to do!"

"You sure you didn't shoot him? Why is he laying like that?"

"He passed out! We were arguing, and he passed out! I didn't shoot him!"

Another moment went by as Jesse continued thinking. Finally he said, "I'm going to check him out. You stay back now, or I'll have to shoot you!"

"Just help him, will you? I don't care if you shoot me! I deserve it, but this man didn't do anything."

Jesse stared at Matt, unconvinced, while wondering if this was some kind of trick to catch him off-guard. He reached out carefully and pulled on the blanket that the baby was on to get him out of the way. After which he looked at Horace and put his hand on his chest. After a moment passed he said, "I think I can feel him breathing! I'm not sure though!

"What would Mr. Simms do?

"I know! I'll call Gerry!"

He said to Matt while walking away backward, "Don't you move now while I get some help! I'm just going into the back room here!"

"I think that door is locked!"

"That's no problem. Just stay where you are at!"

Jesse tried the door and confirmed that it was in fact locked. He didn't lose more than a second or two, however, pulling over the chair that Matt had been sitting on earlier. After standing on it, he felt with his hand along the top of the door frame.

With a smile he exclaimed, "Yep! There it is. I got it!"

He had found a key.

After jumping down, he shoved the chair out of the way and successfully unlocked the door. It opened to a black background that changed to light with the click of a switch. He told Matt to move over where he could continue to watch him, and Matt complied. This led to Jesse backing across the little room and methodically unbolting and unlocking another door. It was a large one, made out of heavy steel.

When he got it opened a little, he proceeded to yell, "Gerry! ...Gerry! ...Hey Gerry, are you back there?"

He became quiet for a moment while listening for a response but soon repeated the name calling in the same way. A faraway cry finally answered in a muted tone, "Alright, I hear you! Just a second, I'm coming!"

Jesse could make out a little form in the distance. It was walking fast and looking larger with each step. A voice called out from it, "What do you need? Gerry isn't here yet!"

Jesse dropped the gun into his pocket, not wanting to startle the guy that was approaching. It clanked into the one he had taken from his brother earlier, and he exclaimed to himself, "Holy shit!"

After which he regained his composure and replied to the guy approaching him, "Gerry's off, oh crap! There's a guy in here that's had a heart attack or something!"

The other fellow, the maintenance man, Charles, replied, "No kidding! Let me see!"

He quickly followed Jesse into the shop. As they looked at the guy and the room, Charles exclaimed, "Whose baby is that?"

"It's Frank's daughter's baby!"

"And who's that guy, the father?"

"No, I don't know who he is, damn it! Can you help this guy lying here or not?"

"No, I can't. We need Gerry!"

Jesse stared at him in disbelief and exclaimed, "You told me that he wasn't in yet! I thought you could help him! You're wasting time! This guy could be dying or something!"

"Let me explain!"

The subject of Jesse's angst looked down at his watch and stated, "With luck Gerry will be coming in any minute now! He's working the late shift!"

Matt interrupted, "What can this guy do that you're talking about?"

Charles and Jesse replied in stereo, "He's a paramedic!"

Jesse added, "Well, he's training to be one. He keeps a medical case here. He's been watching out for Frank and Ben!"

Jesse turned to Charles, saying, "How about if you go and see if Gerry's here yet? If he is, tell him to hurry!"

Charles took off running, after which Jesse looked over at Matt and asked, "What happened that made this guy go out like this?"

"It was my fault. I was accusing him of something. Something I'm now sure he didn't do. I was ready to kill him, but he showed me that I was wrong. Now if he dies, I'll know it was my fault! He probably got so scared that he had a heart attack! I was so stupid! How could I do this? How could I be so wrong?"

This made Jesse think of his brother Ernie's situation. That resulted in his feeling some compassion for Matt. The guy was acting so sorry, so forlorn. He thought, "It's Christmas Eve. No one should feel like that on Christmas Eve!"

"Well, maybe Gerry can help him. He's a pretty sharp guy!"

After which he looked down at the baby and said, "Wow, little baby, you sure are happy considering all of the crazy stuff that's goin' on around here!

"Holy shit! I've got to tell Julie her baby's here, and Mr. Simms too! And they need to know that Frank isn't!"

Looking back up, he said to Matt, "I'm going to get the baby's mom and my friend Mr. Simms. They are worried about what's going on over here! You just sit down and try to relax. I'll be right back!"

As Jesse returned to Ben's shop, he immediately started to explain what was going on across the street. Julie was taking it all in but after seeing a flashing outside the window, exclaimed, "There's the police! Let's go!"

Jesse said, "Hold on a second! Let me tell you something. Frank and your husband aren't over there, but your baby is and it's fine!"

Hearing that, Julie couldn't wait any longer and shot out of the shop and across the street. Jesse had to stay back and assist Ben. As Julie dodged the police car the policeman jumped out and yelled to her, "Hey there you....stop!"

She turned and looked at him while blurting out, "Look, officer, I'm the one that called. My baby is in there!"

The policeman retorted, "Just stop now, right there! I'm ordering you!"

She advanced a few steps and then stopped while crying out to him in frustration, "I just talked with a guy that was in there! Look across the street. Do you see him? He's helping my friend Ben come over. He told me my baby's in there. I've got to get to him!"

The policeman added sincerely in a commanding tone, "Listen, now lady! I got a call that there's someone in this place up to no good! No one's going in until I check it out first!"

She started to reply, "But…"

When out of the darkness a voice called out to her, "Julie, Julie, oh thank God, you're here!"

Julie looked toward him and exclaimed, "Oh, Stash, you're safe! I was so worried about you! We need to get Johnny! Why did you leave him in there?"

As they embraced and Stash started to explain, Ben and Jesse were just getting across the street. Jesse had told Ben what happened, and Ben said in a happy tone to the others, "I can't see you all that well, but Jesse here says that there's a family reunion going on!"

Julie replied, "Well, it will be one once we get our baby!"

After which she focused on Jesse and added, "Could you please tell this policeman that it's ok for me to go inside?"

Jesse responded after facing the policeman, "Officer, you need to go in there in a hurry! Her baby's alright, but there's a guy that looks like he might have had a heart attack or something!"

Mike, the policeman, replied, "Alright, but I have to ask you all to wait out here till I check it out!"

He went in and about a minute later came out and said to Julie, "It's alright! You can go in now, but get your baby and come right back out. There's a paramedic working on the old guy in there, and I'm calling for an emergency vehicle! He's not responding"

Stash asked, "Is that Matt? Which one is it? Is it Matt or Horace?"

Jesse piped in before the policeman could answer, "It's Horace! That's the name of the guy that is sick."

Stash said, while following Julie into the shop, "Oh damn, that's too bad. I thought it was Matt because he was the one that got glass in his hands when the door busted! Horace was looking after our little Johnny! I wonder what happened to him!"

Stash dashed after Julie into the shop and could see Gerry working on Horace. Seeing that Julie was smiling while holding their baby, he asked Gerry, "Is he going to be alright?"

"He's breathing, but otherwise he's not responding. We need to get him to a hospital!"

"When Charles here came and got me, I thought that it was Frank that needed the help!"

Julie reacting to this by crying out, "Frank, did you say Frank? That's my father! Do you know where he is?"

"I'm sorry ma'am, I haven't seen him since yesterday!"

Jesse wanted to see what was going on. He couldn't leave Ben alone though, after the others had hurried into the shop. Ben was of the same mind, so Jesse slowly assisted him following the others. As they entered, they smiled after seeing that Julie was rocking her baby tenderly in her arms. As Stash checked out his son, she asked him, "Honey, where can my father be?"

Stash just looked back at her bewildered and asked, "Father?"

She realized then how absurd her question must have sounded to him and added, "Oh, Stash, I'm so sorry to have done this to you! I should have told you the truth about my dad a long time ago. I was so stubborn! You could have helped me. I know you would have helped me!"

With those words said, she started to cry! Stash tried to console her while the others sympathized with the situation of her father being gone.

As everyone waited for the ambulance to come, Julie explained to Stash about the long separation she had with her father and how it had all started. The story finally ended with her saying that she was so ashamed of not coming back to Chicago long before to sort things out with her dad. She showed Stash a plaque that she had made in a little shop near the train station. It had an inscription that read, "There's no one that I would rather travel to see on Christmas Eve than you, dad!"

Behind the writing was a picture of an old-fashioned steam engine train.

She knew Stash's personality. He was so loving and kind. He would never have let this thing go on as long as it had. She kept it from him for that very reason. When her dad didn't reply to her letters, she was really hurt. Hurt so bad that when Stash asked about her father, she told him that he was dead. Now she really regretted that terrible lie. She worried that something really bad could have happened to him like it had to the poor man that was lying across the table.

CHAPTER EIGHT

A Fork in the Road

It had been a long day for Frank. One filled with bad feelings and recriminations. He was really shaken by Ben's note. This was one time that he knew that the cards were stacked against him. If Ben stopped being his friend it would be the last straw. He couldn't do that to himself, and he surely couldn't do it to Ben.

So he forced himself to read Julie's last letter. She didn't tell him what was wrong, but he knew by the words she had chosen that something very serious was going on. He worried, was she sick, what possibly could it be, that she would write, "Dad, I have to talk to you. It's so important, and we've just got to get past our stubbornness. I fear that this may be the last chance!"

This disturbed him so, that he started to read the other letters, hoping that they might shed some light on it all. They weren't very telling toward the situation at hand. Instead they were filled for the most part with questions about him and Ben and the antique shop.

She would ask in the relative seasons how he had rearranged or decorated the store. There were many that referred to specific regular customers. Did Hank the table man ever find a match to that early New England chair that he always brought in to show off? Was there ever an answer to Burt Benson's request in the paper for a wife? The man was ninety years old and was married five times after he turned seventy. He had said the secret to his longevity was to eat three raw eggs each day. She recalled how her dad had said he would rather be dead.

Julie wondered if Frank had ever discovered the origin of that old book that had just showed up on the bookshelves one day. What was it called, The Legend of Non-A-Me? She had been mesmerized by it. It included a lot of life and moral lessons.

She also asked if anyone ever reopened Sally's Diner. How about her daughter, Kathleen? Did she ever come back and say what she'd been doing since she got married?

Frank remembered how Kathleen had been so nice to Julie. She played such a great part in her adolescent years. With Dorothy gone, there were a lot of times when Frank didn't know how to act with her. Kathleen had a real knack though. Because of that, Julie spent a lot of afternoons and weekends over at the diner. Kathleen let her help out around the place. The extra spending money wasn't as important as the boost it gave to her self-esteem. He considered then how Kathleen and Julie had a lot in common.

After Sally's husband Jim was called up in World War II, she was left with Kathleen as a new baby and the diner to run. She got the news that Jim was killed and was devastated. She would likely have thrown in the towel if she didn't have Kathleen to care for. Somehow she made a go of it.

Kathleen was raised in the diner, and it was the only world she knew. She grew into a woman, and her mom died of cancer in mid-life. Kathleen just pressed on with the business. It was quite a surprise to everyone in the area when she got married and sold the place. Early on she would stop by when shopping downtown. In time though, after seeing that the diner was closed and it stayed that way, she lost heart in visiting anymore.

This led Frank to think about other ways that the neighborhood had changed. Mrs. Dunn had closed down her newspaper stand and gone to live with her son and his wife in Dearborn, Michigan. Vito relocated his barbershop to the north side. Alonzo moved his shoeshine operation to an inside location in Englewood near 63rd and Halsted. His helper Sam had left a couple of years earlier.

The last time Frank saw Kathleen was at Mrs. McGinney's wake and funeral. Her husband missed the wake and funeral because he was on a sales trip to New York. Frank remembered Kathleen commenting that she wished he could have come. She said that Mrs. McGinney was the reason that Kathleen and her husband had gotten together.

She then asked about Joe. Frank told her that the last time he heard from him was before he went into the service. He resisted the temptation to tell her what else he and Ben had discovered then.

The day that Joe enlisted, he came into the antique shop in the evening and found Frank and Ben playing a game of chess. Joe appeared much more talkative than they had ever experienced. Soon they realized that he had tipped back a few. The words just tumbled out like an old woman in a confessional that needed someone to talk to. Joe reflected on how he had worked at the diner since he was seventeen years old.

Back in that teenage time he was joined there by a couple of his friends from 18th Street. They all got a real kick out of having jobs downtown. In their time off they would explore the whole area, the lake, the museums, the restaurants, the hotels, and the Art Institute. They knew what was on each floor of the department stores, they visited all the movie houses, they peered across the lake from the top floor of the Prudential Building, and they got to know the names of a lot of the owners of the shops that dotted the streets. They had ridden all of the subway trains and the "L" and could tell you every bus route that traveled to or around the great matrix of buildings. Downtown was their playground.

As Joe's friends moved on to what they viewed as bigger and better things, he stayed with the diner. His friends knew why he did this, but it was a well-kept secret from everyone else in the area. Joe was hopelessly and completely infatuated with Kathleen. He watched as she bloomed into a lively and beautiful teenager. He would have done anything for her. In his mind and dreams, she was the only answer.

He was in heaven each day working alongside of her, and time seemed to pass in a flash. When she was happy, he was happy, and when she was sad, he tried to perk her up. Like when her mother died and she seemed totally lost to the world. He wanted to save her, to take care of her, to solve all of her problems.

Joe worked and saved and was waiting for just the right moment to tell her how he felt. When she told him one day that she was getting married to the rich guy, he was absolutely and totally crushed. It took every ounce of his unending devotion to accept being the best man at her wedding.

He remained loyal to the end when it was her wish to sell the diner. Stepping up like a good knight he used all of the money he had saved to buy it. The diner, though, without Kathleen was an empty shell. At first he managed to keep up his charade as she visited a few times. He held out hope that she would grow disillusioned with Horace and come back.

When she came in one day with her new baby, the house of cards finally came down, and he knew he had to get away. The army seemed to be the only option that would distance him far enough from Kathleen. Frank and Ben were the only remaining members of the small shop owners that had grouped together near Sally's restaurant, and neither had heard from Joe again. After wondering for a moment if Joe got caught up in the war in Vietnam, his thoughts focused back on Julie.

With all the questions that Julie had asked in her letters, Frank realized that she really missed being in the shop. The questions that affected him most were about the train.

Years earlier when Julie was still quite young, a fellow traded an old but well-made train set for a watch. Normally, Frank would have just displayed the engine and cars in his large glass case, but Julie asked a million questions about the set. _What kind of train was it? Was it like a real one? Then where did the real one go? What were each of the cars called? How come the last car was called a caboose? What did they put in the box cars? If we set the train up with the tracks would the train move? If we went to the train station would we see one like ours?_ It was a never ending subject for her.

Frank figured that he might as well just set up the train. That might be the only thing that would satisfy her! The problem though was that he couldn't dedicate the space that a working train set demanded. That is, until he got an inspiration.

He had always told Julie that an antique dealer needed to feel a special attraction to the pieces that he invested in. If that attachment wasn't there, he probably would fail to do the research needed to make the piece turn a profit.

Contrary to the impression of most laymen, antique dealers don't depend on casual passing shoppers for their living. Folks that just drop in to satisfy their short-term need to see old stuff, hardly ever make a notable purchase. The reason is that they don't have a clue as to what makes the stuff valuable. The information of value was available, but one needed to know where to look.

Frank had recently decided that one of the lines that he displayed, "The old glass bottle group," no longer triggered the excitement in him that it once had. By coincidence there was another dealer interested in taking the whole collection off his hands. He figured to make a tidy sum.

An indication of how he originally felt about the bottles was where he had them displayed. There was a shelf mounted high on the walls that continued all around the room's perimeter, even above the doors. It had been a safe place for the glass vessels, because no one could reach them. The way

Frank felt about them afterward, he would have put the whole lot away in an attic if he had one.

He thought that it was funny that the only ones that didn't get sold were the little medicine bottles. They were hidden from view in the cabinet mounted on the wall behind his desk, and he had forgotten all about them.

With the bottle shelf then being available, it was an ideal place for him to mount the train set for Julie. This way it would be out of the way of valuable displays and the fingers of inquisitive children coming in with their parents. The last thing he wanted was to leave the impression that it was a toy shop.

He considered how he had a hard enough time keeping kids off the antique furniture. There was a special display area for these on a one-step platform adjacent to the back wall. The furniture was his specialty. He was proud of his pieces and this showed because the platform was the only area in the shop that was carpeted. He even roped it off to try to keep the kids from sitting on the chairs. Several times he had to even tell Julie to stay away from those items, and he was hurt to see her disappointment. He knew that she needed things to focus on with her mom gone. When she wasn't in school the shop was the only place that he could keep an eye on her.

So he set up the track on the shelf and used a little imagination by lining the adjacent walls with wallpaper that featured different outdoor scenes. There were mountains and water and fields. He created bridged spaces between the shelves to go over rivers and ravines. There were villages, farms, and even a circus set up with a large tent and all the characters and animals that you would expect to see there. One whole corner was devoted to a forest of evergreens.

Frank got really enthused with the project. He had to buy additional track sections and found in time that there was more available than he needed for the perimeter of the shop. So he made holes through the rear wall to allow the track to extend into the back room too.

This brought forth another inspiration, and Ben helped him build a narrow elevated platform with a handrail that extended along the width of the back room. They made a little ladder so Julie could access it. Finally they capped it all off by installing a long narrow window that Julie could see through from the platform into the main room. That platform became Julie's little train station, and the window was the passage to her imagination. She controlled the whole train layout from up there. She could start and stop the train anywhere along its long run. This allowed her to pretend that the little plastic characters she placed in the various cars were getting on and off.

The train was such a hit with Julie that Frank even bought her a little gray bib overall outfit and hat to imitate that of an engineer. It was only one of many that she wore however. When Kathleen from the diner saw what they had done, she made several colorful costumes for her. Frank could tell by the one she wore on any given day where Julie was planning in her imagination to travel to on the train.

She might become a farm girl or trapeze artist or even a downhill skier. Then maybe a nurse or a teacher or a mother of a clan of unruly children that played too close to the tracks. Sometimes she sold the train tickets and sometimes she was the conductor. Once and awhile she was even the rich and ornery old railroad owner coming out to inspect the station. Many of these characters came from stories that Frank would tell her when they were sitting alone at night. The whole scheme was then reinforced by an old rerun of a little rascal movie that featured them having their own train.

Whatever her role, there was an assortment of dolls that she placed on a little bench on the platform to play other parts. Her imagination was large and vivid in its detail. Frank felt that he had finally done something good for her. The smiles and enthusiasm she demonstrated in her new world showed that she agreed.

When Frank decorated the shop for the various holidays, Julie asked him to add some to the train route and her station too. He was happy to oblige, and they created little schemes that became traditions. For Christmas the train was used to search out and bring back the most perfect Balsam and for Halloween the route was loaded with scary creatures like ghosts, witches, and goblins. His hand now clenched on her Christmas letter of the previous year, where she had asked him, "Dad, do you still decorate the train? Do you still use it to get the perfect tree? I wish I was there doing it with you!"

When Frank read this a little tear developed in the corner of his eye. Try as he might he couldn't stop it. The one was followed by another and soon with a few more words read there was a whole deluge.

He sobbed and laid his head down on his arms while saying, "Honey, why did you have to go? God, I miss you so much!"

This prompted a decision. Someway, somehow, he would see her. He would do it today and admit what he should have years before, that he was a fool for not answering her letters. He was a fool for not coming to see her as she had requested so many times. He was done being a fool. Each day was precious now. He didn't know how many more he would have, and he couldn't waste any of them.

He put on his heavy coat and dropped some cash that was on hand into his pocket. After that he walked out the back of the shop to see Gerry the maintenance -man and paramedic that kindly looked over his and Ben's immediate medical concerns. Gerry though, wasn't by his desk, so Frank wrote him a note and opened a drawer to find an envelope. He put the note in it, wrote Gerry's name on the envelope, and placed it on the desk. After this, he took a shortcut that Gerry had shown him that went through his back door and the maintenance department. It let out at a receiving dock in an alley on the building's other side. From there he headed to the train station.

Once there, he told a ticket agent the town where Julie lived and requested a train that would get him there. There was none. The closest a train could bring him was across the state line. From there he was on his own.

Determined not to be deterred, he bought the ticket anyway. He would find her somehow. As he sat on the southbound train it occurred to him that he hadn't even locked the front door of his shop.

He rationalized, "Well, no one would be coming in on Christmas Eve anyway!"

He would call Ben later and ask him to have Jesse lock up the place. Thoughts of what he would say to Julie filled his head as the train moved steadily out of downtown and through the miles of neighborhoods on the city's southeast side. It wouldn't be long before he would be out in the country.

Frank thought that the worst scenario was that when he reached the station in Indiana that he would have to call a taxi to bring him the rest of the way. He knew that the ride would be expensive, but it didn't really matter. What he wasn't calculating on was how the Christmas Eve holiday would influence the availability of taxis.

When he got to the station and fished through the phone book for a taxi service, only one of those that he had found would answer. That guy made it sound like he would be at the station in about forty-five minutes, so Frank was satisfied. The taxi driver would be picking Frank up on his return trip from another fare going into Illinois. Well, at least that was the plan. The forty-five minutes turned into an hour, an hour and a half, and then two. The time seemed to pass quickly however, because Frank continued to read Julie's letters, some of them more than once.

By the time three hours of waiting had passed, Frank decided that he needed another approach. It had gotten dark, and he could see a little restaurant with a light on across from the station, so he walked over. There he sat at the counter and after ordering some coffee and a sandwich, explained his predicament to the guy running the place.

The man asked customers if there was anyone going Frank's way but there were none. Everyone was in a hurry to join their families. Finally, the man volunteered to take Frank himself because he lived just one town over from where Frank was headed. The only hitch was that Frank would have to wait until the guy closed the place.

Around about eight that evening the same wild weather that ravaged downtown Chicago was whipping up a storm in Indiana. The people there were used to lake-effect snow. It was common for them to get dumped on by more than what fell in the city. Frank thought of it as a mixed blessing because it encouraged the restaurant manager to close the place a little early. With that done though, they had to face driving through the white wet stuff, and it was really coming down!

CHAPTER NINE

Gifts

Once he had made his call for an ambulance, Mike Donovan, the policeman that had answered the call to the antique shop, made his way back inside. As he witnessed the group assembled there, he commented with a grin, "What's the deal here? Is someone handin' out twenty dollar bills? If that's the case, it's my duty to inspect each and every one of them. Been a rash o'counterfeitin' goin' on! I'd be glad to sign a receipt."

With that said he wore a big smile again. It was a much-repeated verse, but he never tired of it. After which he added, "Seriously folks, I've got to make out a report about what happened here. My boss is a stickler for paperwork, or I'd be glad to just get this fellow here cared for and call it a night, bein' Christmas Eve and all. Now who's goin' to step up to the plate and take a swing at it?"

Jesse started to speak up with, "Well, I guess I can fill you in on some of it. You see..."

Suddenly Horace groaned and attempted to sit up! Gerry quickly moved toward him and eased him back down while saying, "Easy there now, fella, don't you worry! We've got help coming!"

It was obvious though to him that Horace was trying to say something. He put his ear down by his face and after a moment said, "Ill, yes, I know you're ill, we're going to help you. Just take it easy! Please relax!"

Horace however, continued with his attempts to speak and Gerry finally yelled out, "Oh pills! Pills?"

Gerry suddenly looked up and while focusing on Jesse asked, "What was he wearing? Did he have a coat on? He must have!"

"Over there! We put his stuff on that counter!"

Gerry went over to it and worked his hands first through the suit coat. When checking the overcoat he exclaimed, "Jackpot!"

After reading the writing on a plastic container, he stated, "These must be what he was asking for!"

Julie spoke up, "Let's get some water and give him one!"

Gerry retorted, "Hold up there ma'am! We don't know how often he takes these! We can't just dispense medicine without some instructions!"

He bent down his head again by Horace and asked him, "Hey there, Mister, can you tell me when you're supposed to take these pills?"

Stash spoke up and said, "It's Horace, his name is Horace!"

Julie looked at him and smiled.

Gerry repeated, "Horace, Horace, can you tell me when you take these pills?"

He again held his ear to Horace's mouth, and this time he said, "I think he's saying 'wallet!' I checked his pocket, but there was nothing there!"

This prompted Matt to lift up his head from his hands and say, "His wallet's on the table!"

Gerry quickly pushed some remaining books to the side and responded, "There's nothing here!"

Jesse exclaimed, "Wait! Look there under the baby blanket!"

Sure enough the wallet was tucked under it. Jesse added, "It must have gotten covered when I moved the baby!"

Gerry looked through the wallet and found a medical card. He read it and said, "Ok, this is good. We can give him a pill. He takes one each day or any time if he has a fainting episode!"

"We need some water, and we'll have to sit him up!"

Charles piped in, "We have a water cooler in the back!"

Matt offered, "There might be some in that cup on the desk."

Jesse checked and confirmed, "Yeah, there is some in here!" Gerry altered his position to get around to Horace's other side and said, "That's good! Here now, someone give me a hand!"

Several of the men rushed forward, but the closest, Charles and Jesse, were all that was needed. As they sat Horace up he opened his eyes. Gerry said to him, "Here you go, Horace! I'm just going to place this on your tongue. Don't bite down."

Gerry put the cup up by Horace's mouth, and he managed to take some and swallow. Gerry told them, "We'll hold him up a minute to make sure he's getting that pill down. Then we'll ease him back onto the table."

"Is that ok, Horace?"

Horace tried to respond but couldn't get out the words. Gerry quickly stated, "I'm sorry, Horace! It's ok. You don't have to say anything."

Mike the policeman interjected, "Well, things are looking up here now! How about if we continue where we left off?"

He looked over at Jesse and added, "I believe you were going to tell me something! How about if you start with this fellow's name? I heard the first was Horace, but how about lookin' in his wallet there and telling me his last name? I've got to get the details, you know."

Matt looked up again as Jesse picked up the wallet and found a credit card inside.

"It's Williams, Horace Williams.

A note of familiarity with the name swelled up through the crowd, but at that moment with none any more than Mike himself. He exclaimed, "Jesus, Mary, and Joseph, I've got to check this out!"

He pulled a little pad from his pocket as his face brightened and he asked Horace, "Would you sir, be the Horace Williams with a wife Kathleen, and I must say it's a beautiful name, the same as my own lovely wife. And would you reside at an address in Lincoln Park? Now all you have to do is move your head a little for either a yes or a no."

Horace managed to shake his head to the affirmative and Mike shouted, "Oh sweet Mary, I've hit the mother load! Wait until the lieutenant hears this. I'll get a promotion!"

With that he smiled and winked at Charles who was standing closest to him. After that he said to Horace, "Do you know, Mr. Williams, that your wife, Kathleen, has half of the department lookin' for you tonight? I heard that she's the one that looked after sweet Mrs. McGinney, the angel of Wabash Street!"

While turning he added, "I'll be back in a minute, folks. I've got to call this in!"

As Mike left the shop, Julie rushed up by Horace and asked,

"Do you remember me, Horace? I'm Julie! I was the flower girl at your wedding!"

Horace looked at her and showed a little smile. He reached out and put his hand on hers. It was obvious that he was regaining his composure when he said to her, "You've got a great little guy there, Julie. He hardly fussed at all. Just one bottle and a diaper! He's a little trooper."

Then he closed his eyes for a moment. Julie turned and exclaimed to Stash, "I've got to call Kathleen! She must be so worried!"

Gerry spoke up, "I'm sure the police will notify her!"

Julie retorted, "I know though how she must feel! I'm going to call her, just in case their call is delayed!"

A Christmas Reckoning

She added excitedly while rifling through a desk drawer, "Oh my, where's the phone book? It should be in the bottom drawer!"

Just then a siren blared and lights flashed outside the building. More sirens could be heard as a fire truck was also rushing up to where the other vehicle had stopped. Mike put down his phone, got out of his squad car, and greeted the fire department personnel coming onto the scene. Soon there were several men coming into the shop with their equipment.

Julie found the book and the number she was seeking and asked Stash for the cell phone. He gave it to her, but said, "Honey, when I tried it earlier, it didn't work in the shop. You should go outside!"

"Well, ok, you take Johnny, and I'll go make the call!"

When she got outside Mike was back in his squad car and could be seen talking on his phone. She thought that maybe he had beat her to the punch, so she just stood near the car waiting for him to finish. After he got off the phone, Mike was still occupied by some paperwork and didn't notice her. So she knocked lightly on his window. Surprised, he opened it and said, "I'm sorry there, missus! What can I help you with?"

"I was just checking to see if you reached Horace's wife, Kathleen. I'm sure she would be relieved to know where Horace is!"

"I called it in and left a message, but I'm not sure just how long it will take. The phones are swamped at the station with everything that's been happening tonight. It's a procedure for them to call though, so don't worry! It's just a matter of time!"

"If it's alright, I would like to give her a call myself! Would that be alright?"

"Why sure there, missus! It's a free country, and why don't you sit in the back and get out of the cold! It's awful out there!"

Julie smiled and did as he suggested. Once seated, she dialed, and the phone only rang twice when someone answered with a hesitant, "Hello."

Julie asked, "Kathleen, is that you?"

The voice at the other end replied, "Yes, and who is this?"

"This is Julie, Frank's daughter from the antique shop, do you remember me?"

"Oh my, why of course, Julie, what a nice surprise! Julie honey, I would love to talk to you now, but I'm waiting for an important call!"

"I know Kathleen, that's why I'm calling you! Horace is alright! He's here with us at the antique shop!"

"Oh my God, you say he's there! He's alright! I was so worried and…"

Julie could hear her sobbing and tried to console her with, "He's fine now Kathleen, don't cry. He's ok. It's been quite a night for him, but he's fine now."

In front of the car, a little tear formed in Mike's eye as he overheard what Julie was saying. He caught it before it dripped, with a finger in his black imitation leather glove.

Kathleen then questioned, "You say he's alright now! Was he hurt?"

"No, he wasn't hurt! He apparently fainted, but when he was given one of his pills, he started to perk right up! There's an emergency unit here, and they are checking him over, but he looks like he's coming around just fine!"

Kathleen sobbed again and stated sadly, "I did this to him! I should have never said that I was leaving to see our daughter. He misunderstood and thought I was divorcing him! I feel so terrible!"

Julie heard more sobbing and added compassionately, "He's alright, Kathleen, you would really be proud of him! He watched over my baby when my husband and I lost track of each other today. I was so surprised when I discovered that he even gave him a bottle and changed him!"

"Horace changed your baby's diaper? That doesn't sound like him! Are you sure that's my Horace?"

"Yes, and not only that! My husband told me that the store's glass door shattered and this other fellow got a lot of it on him! Horace helped pick the glass out of the man's hands, and he covered the door where the glass broke to keep the cold out! He's had a very busy night!"

All Kathleen could reply to this was, "Oh my Lord! I can't believe it. My Horace did all that?"

After forcing herself to regain some composure Kathleen asked, "Julie, can he talk? Can I speak to him, please?"

"Well, not just yet, but soon! I'm sorry but this darned old cell phone won't work inside the shop. I'm calling from a police car! I'm sure that he will be able to talk to you as soon as he's able to come outside. I don't know if the paramedics are going to bring him to a hospital to be checked out further or what! As soon as he's outside though, I'll make sure he talks to you! It'll just be a little while, ok?"

"Ok, honey, thanks so much for calling and when we get the chance, I would love to catch up with how you and Frank and Ben and all the others are doing. It's been so long!"

Julie thought about her dad and a sad wave came over her, but she replied, "Yes, Kathleen that will be great. I'll talk to you soon!"

When she got off the phone, she called up to Mike asking,

"Sir, sir, can I ask you a question?"

"Why sure, ma'am, what is it?"

"I called the police earlier to ask for help because I was concerned for the safety of my father! When we came in though, he wasn't there. I'm so worried about him and I was wondering if you could help me find him?"

"Oh my goodness ma'am, I assumed, when I saw the other fella sitting in there that he was the guy that was missing! Who is that one?"

Julie thought about that for a second and replied, "I really don't know! My husband said that he and Horace were both in the shop when the door busted. That guy was the one who got showered with the glass. I have no idea who he is though!"

"I've got to go back inside, missus. Don't worry now, we'll find your father, but this other fellow who was hurt, he must have a family that's waitin' to hear from him too!"

"Oh, for heaven's sake, that's right! It didn't occur to me, that poor man!"

Mike said, as he opened his door, "Once and for all, I've got to get the whole story on what has happened here! All I can say is that this is one heck of a Christmas weekend!"

Meanwhile, Gerry was busy filling in the paramedics on what had appeared to have happened to Horace and Matt. Horace was pretty alert by that point and said to him, "I really want to thank you for helping me, son. If I didn't get that pill, I could have slipped into a coma."

Matt spoke up too, with, "Yes, thanks for helping me too! My hands stopped throbbing with whatever you put on them!"

Stash added, "Hey, that goes for me to!"

Gerry responded to them, "You're all welcome, but you should get those wounds checked out at a hospital. I picked out some of the remaining glass, but the light's not good enough in here to be sure that I got all of it."

Charles was observing this and couldn't help having some cynical thoughts float through his mind.

"Go ahead. Why don't you just take a bow? There wouldn't be any light on at all in here if I didn't get the emergency generator on! C'mon now, Gerry, I've got to get back to check on Elsie!"

As if he read his mind, Gerry looked over at him and said, "C'mon Charles, we need to get back now!"

Charles quickly followed him out through the rear door. As they walked down the hall, approaching the maintenance department, Charles commented to Gerry, "How come you've got Smitty working tonight? I didn't expect to see him on Christmas Eve!"

Gerry abruptly stopped and looked at Charles strangely while saying, "Have Smitty working?"

"Well, yah, he's in your office. He's been in there all night! I walked by after the power went out, and I turned the generator on! He waved and smiled at me."

For a moment, Gerry took this all in. After which he put his hands squarely on Charles' shoulders and while looking eye to eye with him stated, "First thing, Charles, that's Mr. Smithers, not 'Smitty'! He doesn't like being referred to that way!"

"Fine, I just heard a couple of the other guys say..."

"I know what they say, but don't you."

Charles got a funny look after hearing that and said, "Oh, not me huh, why not?"

Gerry sensed the tone of his question and answered, "I know which guys you are talking about, and they don't give a damn about their jobs. I had gotten the impression though, that you take your job very seriously!"

"I do!"

"Well, the second thing you should take in now is that Mr. Smithers doesn't report to me!"

"No? I just thought because he shares your office sometimes..."

Gerry cut him off again by saying, "He comes down to my office to get a close look at what's going on in maintenance. He does the same thing with all of the other service groups."

"I don't understand! How come?"

"Because he's my boss and the boss for all of them! He's the superintendent of the whole building!"

"Superintendent, you're kidding! But he's bla..."

Gerry interrupted him again while giving a wide-eyed look and said, "Yes... so what's your point?"

Charles was finally seeing the light and all he could say was, "Wow!"

"Right, now you are finally getting it!"

As they got to the maintenance department, Gerry stopped again and said to Charles, "So it was you that turned on the generator. How long did it take you?"

"About half a minute!"

"Hey, that's great! That's gotta be some kind of a record. Good job!"

"Thanks, man!"

"Look, I'll be back in a couple of minutes. I've got to talk to Mr. Smithers about something."

Charles looked surprised and asked with concern, "Not about me I hope!"

"No, don't worry Charles; this is a subject that I talked to Mr. Smithers about a long while back!"

Meanwhile, in the antique shop, Horace had motioned for Jesse to come over, and the two talked quietly for awhile. After which the emergency personnel came up by Horace again and suggested that he go to the hospital, but he declined this adamantly, saying, "No, I'm fine! All I needed was my pill. I feel like a million dollars now! You can't imagine how good I feel!"

The paramedic discussed this with his partner and told Horace, "I have to call the hospital! I'll be back to check on your vitals again in a couple of minutes."

In the meantime, Mike approached Matt and was getting some personal information like his name and address. Both Horace and Jesse were listening to the questions intently. Mike finally looked over and asked Jesse, "How about explaining to me what happened here?"

Horace spoke out suddenly, "Pardon me, officer. With all respect for this young fellow here, he wasn't in the place to witness a great deal of what happened. I am probably in the best position to tell you!"

Matt just stared up at Horace, staying silent. He thought to himself, "Well, this is it!"

Mike replied to Horace after considering his point, "Certainly it's best for me to get all of the facts, so if you're able, go ahead!"

Horace went into great detail to tell everything that happened. That is, he told everything except all the negative exchanges between Matt and himself. He ended by describing how he had fainted on the baby and thanked God now that Matt was there to pull him off.

Matt just stared at Horace with amazement. With that, Mike directed another question at Matt and Jesse, "How about you two fellows? Do you have anything to add about after Horace here fainted?"

Jesse spoke up quickly, "No, there really isn't much to add. I had come over and heard Matt yelling for help. I came in and because I knew that the maintenance department had a door that could be accessed from the rear, I called for Gerry. Charles actually came first and then Gerry. I think you know the rest!"

Matt looked at Jesse and a tear formed in his eyes. He looked back at Horace and found him smiling. The tears wouldn't stop, and he brought his hand up instinctively to his eyes, but the bandages wouldn't allow him to absorb them. Julie, seeing this, removed a hanky from her purse and walked over to wipe them. Her intuitive sense told her that something bigger was going on than what had been told.

About this same time, Gerry had come back to the shop and told Charles, "Hey, Mr. Smithers wants to talk with you."

"But you said that you wouldn't tell him!"

"I didn't, Charles. This is about me! Today's my last day. In fact, Mr. Smithers told me I could leave and recoup what's left of my Christmas Eve!"

"You're leaving—why? Did he fire you?"

"No, it's nothing like that! I'm the one that quit! I saw tonight that I can do more as a paramedic than I can here. The only reason I was sticking around was for Frank and Ben. I don't know what happened to Frank, and I sure hope he's alright! I realized though that I could be of more help to people like him if I'm out on calls!"

"But look how you helped all those people tonight!"

"I wouldn't have been ready though if this wasn't my passion! Up till today, my main worry was if I could handle the job without someone looking over my shoulder. Now I know that I can!"

Gerry added then with emphasis, "You better go and talk with Mr. Smithers before he leaves!"

Charles held out his hand to shake Gerry's and said, "Good luck, man. It's been nice workin' with you!"

Back in the antique shop, Ben stood in the shadows taking everything in the best that he could. He was happy that Julie and Stash were reunited with their baby and that Horace and the guy named Matt were alright, but his recriminations about Frank continued. He wondered, "Where is he? C'mon Frank, give us a call or somethin', please! We can work things out!"

He couldn't help but think that his note to Frank had led to something bad happening. Jesse came over by him and said, "Mr. Simms?"

Ben looked at him and replied, "I know what you want to talk to me about Jesse. You want to start your own business. I'm sorry, but I just can't sell the shop to you! I couldn't live with myself!"

Jesse was disappointed with this, but he wanted to remain upbeat knowing Ben's concern about Frank. He replied, "That's alright, Mr. Simms, but actually that's not why I walked over. I know you are worried about Frank. I'm sure they'll find him. Julie told me that the policeman made a call, and they are looking for him just like they were for Horace!"

"That is good news, Jesse! It does make me feel a little better. I just wish I knew where to look for him!"

Jesse continued to stand by him and finally he asked Ben, "Aren't you tired of standing here, Mr. Simms? I can take you back across the street! I looked out and the lights are back on over there. The power must have come back on."

"That does sound like a good idea. I just want to stay, though, as long as Julie's here. I know she's scared to death for Frank. I wish I knew how to console her!"

"I don't know how to explain it, Mr. Simms, but I really think that Frank's ok. There's something special going on in here tonight. It's almost magical!"

Ben mumbled to himself, "Ah, for the faith of the young and innocent!"

Jesse asked, "What was that, Mr. Simms?"

"Oh, it's nothing, Jesse! Just that I want to tell you, well, you're a fine young man, and I've really enjoyed working with you!"

"Thanks, Mr. Simms, I appreciate that. I really do!"

There was a lull and Ben added, "Jesse, I feel that I need to explain about my decision!"

"That's not necessary, Mr. Simms. I know that you're really attached to your shop. Honestly, I understand! If it was mine, I doubt that I would give it up either!"

"No, you don't understand, Jesse! I'd give you the place in a minute if it wasn't for the damned tobacco!"

Jesse started to interrupt, but Ben help up a hand and added, "Now wait, son. Let me explain! I need to tell you about something that happened to me recently."

Jesse, in respect for Ben, just listened.

So Ben continued with, "Just last week on Tuesday, around mid-morning, a young woman came into the store. She reminded me of my wife, Margelie, when she was that age. She walked up to the counter and asked for a carton of cigarettes. I don't know why, but I started to quiz her. I said, 'You don't look old enough to buy cigarettes,' even though I actually thought she was.

"She quickly showed me her license, and I said, 'How do I know this is real?' She was looking upset, but she dug into her purse and fished out some other ID's. I looked over them real slow, purposely stalling! Finally I said, 'Well, I don't believe any of this! You look too young to me!'

"Then she says to me, 'Listen, mister, I had to take two busses out of my way to get here. You have the best prices for cartons. You've gotta sell one to me!'

"I just walked over to the register and pulled out three dollars and laid them on the counter. I told her directly, 'Here, this will get you back to where you came from. Now don't come to my shop again!' She got a little tear in her eye and reluctantly took the money in her hand and replied, 'You're nuthin' but a mean old man!' With that she turned around and left!"

After a dwell, Ben added, "You see, Jesse, that girl has her whole life ahead of her, just like you do! That damned tobacco is killin' folks, and I just can't be a part of it anymore. I couldn't sell it to her, and I can't sell the shop so you would do it either. I made a promise to God a few minutes ago that I would stop forever. I just hope that he will bring Frank back safe to me and Julie!"

Seeing that he had finished, Jesse replied emphatically with, "I don't want to sell tobacco either, Mr. Simms! The only reason that I didn't mention it was because I thought you wanted to keep the shop the way it is. My dream is to have a little restaurant where I can sell Mexican food. I hoped to convince you sometime to let me try it for a while before your lease expired. All I need is a place to work out some of my ideas. If they worked, my plan was to move to the south side. There's an area that looks good to me in the Back of the Yards. Property is less expensive there, and I think the neighborhood is going to turn around like it has in Bridgeport!"

Ben was really surprised by all of this and slowly developed a large smile. He replied with emphasis, "Jesse, the shop is yours!"

Jesse looked amazed and exclaimed, "Really, Mr. Simms, are you sure?"

"Jesse, I haven't been this sure of anything in a very long time!"

CHAPTER TEN

His Answer

Charles rushed through the hall right up to the foreman's office where Mr. Smithers was working. He knocked, and Jim waved him in. Charles opened the door and quickly stated, "I'm sorry, Mr. Smithers, I would have been here sooner, but I spotted the indicator light in the shop that showed the power came back on. I knew I better switch back from the generator power so all the systems would be energized."

"That's fine, Charles. I thought that might be what you were doing. That's the kind of attention to what's important that I like!"

Charles had to fight back a smile. He wanted to appear as having a serious work demeanor like Gerry had. After a short pause, Jim continued with, "Charles, did Gerry tell you that he was leaving us?"

"Yes, he did that before he told me to come and see you."

"Good, good, then you know that some extra effort is going to have to be made while I go about filling his position?"

"Yes, I expected that. I'll do my part. You can be confident that the second shift will keep humming along. I've learned a lot from Gerry."

"I'm sure it will, but as you know I need for all the shifts to run smooth."

"Yes, for sure!"

But he didn't know where Mr. Smithers was going with this.

Jim paused again and said, "Charles, Gerry first approached me about leaving three months ago!"

"Oh, really! Wow!"

Jim continued with, "Yes, that's the kind of forethought that I expect from a lead foreman. At that time, I asked him to recommend someone if there was anyone on staff that would make a good replacement. He took some time to get back to me, but when he did, he told me there was not.

"He also said, however, that the second shift didn't have a foreman, but you could be depended on to keep things going pretty well. In fact, I've learned through the years that there's more work on the second shift for maintenance than the others. Gerry has served as the lead foreman and also the foreman on the first shift. Then Jim Verdin is the foreman of the third shift, but Gerry says he's getting along in age and isn't looking for any more responsibility.

"I asked Gerry, 'Well, are you suggesting that we advertise for the position?' He surprised me then with what he suggested. He recommended you for the job!"

Charles responded with shock, "Me?"

"Yes, that was also my first reaction. He, however, cited a whole litany of examples where you were not only willing but proved to be very capable! With that, I started to make note of your performance, and I have not been disappointed. The way you handled the power outage today was the last tally I needed to make my decision. I want you to be our lead foreman!"

Charles' head was swimming. He just couldn't believe this was happening. He came back to reality just as Jim added; "Now, son, you need to know that one of your first hurdles will be to find someone that will take your place on the second shift. Do you think you can handle that?"

"Yes, Mr. Smithers, I'll have personnel place an ad first thing on Tuesday when they are back to work!"

With that Jim smiled and then stood up and held out his hand to Charles while saying, "Congratulations!"

Charles took his hand and grasped it firmly like his momma had taught him years ago, and he replied enthusiastically, "Thank you, sir, thank you very much!"

Jim added as Charles turned to leave, "Oh and Charles?"

"Sir!"

"With your new position you will find a significant increase on your next check, and because you are now on staff you will also qualify for a bonus."

He thought with amazement, "Holy shit, I'm getting a bonus too!" Then said, "Thanks again Mr. Smithers, you've really made my Christmas!"

Before he could turn away though, Jim started yet again with, "Oh, and Charles could you do me a favor? Would you see if you can catch Gerry before he leaves and give him this? It was underneath the mail on my desk!"

"Sure!"

He took the envelope out of Jim's hand and after leaving the office, ran toward the locker room to see if Gerry was still in the building.

At this same time, an old Ford pick-up was plodding through large drifts of snow on the farm roads of Northern Indiana. Frank was assisting his Good Samaritan driver by continually wiping the condensation from the inside of the windshield. Three times they had been stopped by drifts too large to get through and then had to backtrack. If the road stayed open this time, though, they were on the final stretch.

The driver, Phil, had only one worry and that was, "I hope the bridge will be open!"

If it wasn't, Frank would have to give up reaching his destination that night. Phil had already offered to let him stay at his place.

As they caught sight of the bridge and a flashing light, Frank thought the worst. When they approached, though, they could see that it was just a caution light, and there was nothing to impede their momentum. After crossing, Phil breathed a sigh of relief and then stated that it was a good thing that they didn't have to slow down, or they would have never made it over the hill. This was true. Especially the first 40 feet or so of the snow-packed surface had spots with the ice polished like glass from vehicles spinning their tires.

They entered town, and thankfully, Phil knew the area, because as was the case in Chicago, most of the street signs were coated with snow. Phil made a few turns on side streets and all of a sudden came to a stop in front of a large old Victorian-style building. Frank could see a ramp leading to the top of its wrap-around front porch. There was a sign above the porch, but he couldn't make it out. The numbers on the mailbox, however, matched those on the envelope that he held in his hand.

Phil said that he would wait while his traveling companion checked the place out. Frank responded by thanking Phil sincerely. To that he added his concern that the Good Samaritan would be able to get back over the bridge. Phil told him that his brother lived in town and his truck had four-wheel drive. If he needed to he would stop there but thought that he would make it home alright.

Frank got out, waved back to Phil, and approached the building. As he got up close he could see the sign clearer, but the only letters not covered with snow were HOS. He wondered what it meant but decided to advance up the ramp and knock on the door. No one answered, and he tried again with the same result. He looked down and saw the door had an old-time thumb depress handle, and he tried it. Sure enough it opened freely. He hurried inside and shut it behind him firmly against the gusting wind.

He turned back around and was pleasantly surprised by the view that reminded him of an early 1900's vintage hotel. There was a little parlor to the left and to the right a curved counter at the base of a large open staircase that obviously led to a second level. He approached the counter and saw a little sign by a button that read, "Ring For Service."

So he did.

In about half a minute he heard steps on the hardwood floor. A door in a hall behind the counter opened and a large black woman in a white uniform came toward him.

She asked kindly, "Yes, can I help you?"

"It seems that I'm in the wrong place! Before I leave though, could you look at the address on this envelope and tell me how I might get to it? The number seems right, but it must be the wrong street."

She took the envelope from him and quickly replied, "Well, you got the right address, but I don't know any Julie Fleming."

"Are you sure that this is the right street?"

"Yes, I'm sure, and not only that, this looks like one of our envelopes."

She thought for a moment and added, "Now you wait just a second, and I'll check this out with Miss Trudy. She's been here longer than me. Let's see if she knows that name."

The woman left through the same door that she had come in from. In a few seconds she returned and said, "She's not back there. I'll have to look for her upstairs."

As she struggled with the incline she lamented, "I sure do wish we had an elevator. My legs are hurtin' to beat all!"

Back in the maintenance department locker room of the building that held the antique shop, Jesse had found that Gerry was gone. He stood in front of a bench there while thinking, "Wow, what a wonderful and crazy day! Who would have thought that I would start earlier as a mechanic and end by being the lead foreman? I sure wouldn't have!"

He looked down at the envelope and wondered if it was important. He thought, "If this is work related, it could be something I need to know!"

After which it occurred to him, "But Gerry's name is on it!"

He quickly countered that though with, "Hey, I'm the boss now, and a boss is no good if he can't make decisions!"

So he opened the envelope and found the note from Frank. He thought, "Frank, who's Frank? We don't have a Frank working in maintenance. And why does it say for him to tell Ben something? We don't have a Ben either!"

Suddenly a revelation illuminated his mind and he exclaimed, "Holy crap!"

After which he took off running.

As he continued down the hall toward the foreman's office he was suddenly aghast and stopped in his tracks at seeing Elsie there opening the door. He was tempted to yell for her to stop but knew that it was too late. He started walking slowly in the office direction while thinking, "Oh, shit! The cat's out of the bag now!"

He approached the office much slower then, worrying that everything he had recently gained would now be lost. Reaching the door he hesitated but then grabbed the handle. It opened to Mr. Smithers still sitting at the desk with Elsie now standing to his side and staring up at him. Charles started to talk, but Jim signaled for him to stop, while stating, "Wait just a second now, Charles! Your little girl was just telling me all about why she is here."

Elsie continued in her innocent little voice recounting the story of how her daddy was keeping his promise to take her to see the manger scene. When she finished, Jim dwelled for a moment and said, "Well, where I really frown on children being bought to the workplace, and I don't ever expect it to happen again, I am a man who understands the importance of a promise. Especially one made from a parent to a child. So you and little Elsie here should be leaving now if you hope to get to that manger scene. As we talked earlier, I expect to see you here with bells on, Charles, after the holiday break!"

"I will, Mr. Smithers, I certainly will! Thank you again!"

But he remembered, "The letter!"

He unfolded the paper and quickly explained to Jim what was going on with the man named Frank that was lost!

Jim, while quickly grasping the importance of it, exclaimed, "Frank, Frank Fleming from the antique shop, is lost? That letter explains where he is? Hurry up now and bring them the news!"

Charles said to Elsie, "C'mon, honey! We've got to hurry!"

Jim interjected, "You run ahead! Elsie and I will follow you!"

With that Charles took off running again. In what seemed to him like an eternity of running he finally reached the rear entrance of the antique shop. He threw open the door and continued his rush into the front room. His sudden explosive entrance shook everyone from their trances while Charles yelled out, "I know where he is!"

Mike yelled back to counter him, "Hold on there now, tiger! You know where who is?"

He replied enthusiastically, "Frank, the guy Gerry was looking after!"

Julie cried out, "My father, you know where my father is?"

She rushed over to him adding in a desperate tone, "Tell me, please! Tell me!"

Ben piped in, "Yeah, tell us! Where's Frank?"

Charles handed the letter to Julie and said, "Here, read this!"

Julie grasped the letter and after she rushed through the lines, exclaimed, "Oh my God, he's gone to see me!"

Mike queried, "Just a second there, let me see that letter. What do you mean he's gone to see you? You're standing right here! Is he coming here?"

Stash spoke up with, "What I think she means is that he's gone to our home in Indiana. Is that right, honey?"

"Yes, but that means he went out into this storm! How in the world would he get there? He can't drive, and there's no public transportation to our town!"

The room got silent again as everyone considered the possibilities, most of which were bad, until Mike spoke up with, "Look here now, let's not be losing hope! I'll call in and have our guys check out things on the southeast side. They can also make a call to the state police in Indiana and to the local police in your town and the towns near it. If there were any calls to their stations, we'll find out."

With that he went quickly out to his car. In a few minutes he came back in, and Julie asked, "Did you hear something about my father?"

"I'm sorry, missus, not yet. I'm sure we'll be finding out somethin' soon though! I've put the word out."

Just as he was saying this, Jim walked into the room with Elsie. He was bending over a little so he could hold her hand—which also held an open package of Chuckles candy. They had discovered that the red ones were the favorites of both of them, but Jim was quite satisfied to take an orange one as a second choice.

Mike looked over at Matt and said, "Mr. Miller, I do have some news for you, however. I just got word back that your missus is coming out right now to get you!"

Matt looked up at him and replied, "No, there must be some mistake? I haven't…"

Mike cut him off, though, with, "Is your wife's name, 'Marge Miller?'"

"Yes, but…"

Mike cut him off again with, "Well, our office contacted her and told her what happened to you, and she is one determined woman. They told her to wait and we would get you home, but she insisted on coming down here herself!"

Matt fell into thought for a moment and said softly, "Marge!"

"But what about the storm?"

"Oh, I don't think you need to worry about that. I wouldn't let the little lady drive in this, so I sent a car for her."

Matt could hardly take it in. He said to him, with words that were hard to get out, "You did?"

"Sure enough! I figure they're just about fifteen minutes away by now."

To which Matt asked, with his eyes tearing, "How can I ever thank you?"

He followed this by looking around the room at several smiling faces and added, "How can I thank you all?"

To that Mike replied, "Well, if it is me speaking, and it is, I say it's all in a night's work! Just one more to go, and I can call it a night! And what a night it's been! Yes, sir!"

And with that he winked over at Julie, who tried her best to return a smile. She had been busying herself by returning scattered books to the shelves. It was awkward because she refused to set Johnny down again. Suddenly it occurred to her, "What if somehow dad did make it there? I've got to call! I've got to tell them he could be coming!"

She handed the baby to Stash again in a sudden rush and said, "I've got to call home!"

She headed for the door, and Mike spoke up with concern, "Now go easy there, missus, before you slip on the ice and have an accident. Here, I'll walk you out!"

He offered her his arm, and she took it while forcing a smile. Once again when they were outside he suggested that she sit in his car, and she thankfully accepted. She dialed the number and heard the phone ring several times with no answer.

At the other end, Frank listened and watched as the old-style phone vibrated in its base. Finally it stopped ringing. Several seconds went by, and the phone started ringing again. A voice from up the stairs called out, "Could you be a dear and get that please? I'll never get down these stairs on time!"

So Frank reached over and grabbed the phone and said, "Hello?"

Hearing a man's voice, Julie replied, "Oh, I'm sorry! I must have gotten the wrong number!"

"Please, miss, don't hang up! I'm just answering the phone for the woman here. It's taking her a minute to get down the stairs!"

Julie paused for a second and replied, "Ok, thank you, I'll wait."

Suddenly it dawned on her. She yelled into the phone, "Wait, please!"

Frank answered, "Ok, I'll wait! What's the matter, she's almost here?"

"Dad, dad, is that you?"

"No, ma'am, this is Frank. Just wait one second!"

This made Julie start to cry, and she called out emotionally,

"Dad, please listen to me! Stay on the phone! It's Julie, your daughter!"

There was a short pause, and Julie could hear Frank say, "Julie, did you say Julie?"

Julie replied while sobbing, "Yes, daddy, it's me!"

She could hear him say to someone, "Oh my God, it's my daughter, Julie!"

He exclaimed into the phone, "Julie, Julie, honey, where are you? They said that I'm at the address on your letter!"

"My letter, you read my letter?"

"Yes, honey, I read all of them! I've been such an old fool. I want to be with you, honey, wherever you are at!"

Through more tears and sobs she just managed to eke out, "Oh, daddy, I want to be with you too!"

Frank replied awkwardly, "Just a second, honey, this woman here is insisting that she talk to you!"

"It's ok, daddy. I know her. Just stay close by."

The woman got on the phone and after talking for a moment, Julie said, "Vela, could you talk to me in the back room please?"

So Vela told Frank that she had to check something in back for Julie, and she hit a button on the phone base and hung it up. In a minute she got back on and after listening, Julie cried out, "Oh no, not now! Please Lord, not now!"

Mike was startled by this and called out, "What's the matter, missus? I thought you found him!"

Julie got control over herself, put her hand on the phone, and replied in a calmer tone, "I'm sorry, officer! It's alright. I did find him, and he's ok. Could you tell the others, please?"

"Oh, alright, missus, I think that's what I'll do."

With that he left the car.

After a few more minutes of talking with Vela, Julie asked Vela to put her back on with her dad. She did and Julie said, "Hi, daddy! I'm sorry that I made you wait. Let me tell you about some of the wild and wonderful things that have been happening!"

"Ok, but where are you? I want to see you! Are you close by?"

"Daddy, I know you are going to find this hard to believe, but I'm at your shop!"

"My shop? Oh my Lord, how did you get there?"

Julie set about telling Frank about her husband, Stash, and her little miracle baby that she gave birth to when she was forty-six years old. How up to then she had lost hope of ever having a child. That was why she and Stash named him John, just like the baby of Elizabeth and Zechariah in the Bible. Frank was thrilled to discover he was a grandfather. He was also amused to hear that Stash worked for the railroad. He asked then if Julie had ever become a nurse as she had discussed in her early letters, and she confirmed that she had.

Finally she talked of all the crazy happenings of that day and night at the antique shop. He was completely bowled over by it all and when she finished the story she added, "Now, daddy, I told Vela to take good care of you. She's going to prepare a room there for you to spend the night. Stash and I will get back there with the first train in the morning. Vela will come and pick us up from the station."

Her dad thanked her, and they said a very happy and heartfelt goodbye.

Julie then came inside the shop, and everyone crowded around her as she took little Johnny from Stash again and then hugged the two of them. The others quizzed her, and she talked happily about her father, and everyone basked in the joy that came from it all. In the process, Ben hugged her and so did all the rest.

As they spread out, Julie laid the baby down on the table to change him, and Stash looked over them like the proud father that he was. The others crowded back to each side, and some stood up on tippy-toes and looked over shoulders to share the view of the little guy.

Elsie cried out, "I want to see the baby too!"

With that, Jim lifted Elsie up high and sat her on his shoulders. He said to her, "How's that, sweetheart? Can you see him now?"

Everyone looked up at her with smiles. She suddenly called out happily with a look of wonder on her face, "I can see everything now! It's the manger scene just like daddy told me. There's Mary and Joseph and the little baby Jesus! There are shepherds and wise men, and there are angels everywhere!"

They all looked at each other and laughed and smiled at her observation. Julie focused upward and said to her sweetly, "It is kind of like a manger scene, isn't it, with everyone looking at the baby? I can see everyone but the angels. But you know, I see one now, and its you!"

Elsie replied, "There are angels, they're all around us! Don't you see them? Look up there. Some of them are playing with the train!"

Julie did look up and happily rediscovered the playthings of her youth. Just then there was a wrrrr sound, and the train came to life. It started moving around the track slowly until it abruptly stopped at the circus. It dwelled there for a moment, but soon advanced until it made another stop by the raging river. Yet again it started and went around the room till it arrived at the evergreen tree forest. Everyone in the room was fixated on its motion, and Julie spoke up excitedly, "That's where daddy and I would get our Christmas tree!"

She wondered about what she had just witnessed and called out, "Daddy, daddy, are you in the station?"

She stopped short, though, and caught herself with, "What am I saying? He can't be there! He's in Indiana. What's going on? Who's running the train?"

She got up and handed little Johnny to Stash and then ran to the back room. In a moment she came back to the doorway with a puzzled look exclaiming, "There's no one in there!"

Jesse piped in, "Maybe the electricity went back on!"

Charles replied, "No, that's not it, the electricity has been back on for a while now."

Jim interjected, "Well maybe the train was just hung up for some reason."

Gerry, who had forgotten his bag, had come back into the room just in time to see the train's peculiar movements. He took a turn in the reactions by agreeing with Jim, "Yeah, it must be something like that!"

Matt questioned, "But why did it stop at those different places?"

Jim offered, "Well, maybe there are little switches in those spots making it do that!"

Julie piped in, "No, that's not the way it works. I controlled it from my station on the platform!"

They were all silent once more. Again the train started, and this time it continued on its return route into the back room.

Julie added, "I can remember playing for hours and hours with that train! I went on journeys to wonderful places with all of my imaginary friends."

Elsie asked her, "Do you see the angels now?"

Julie answered, "Well, not now, but I think I saw some back then!"

"You need to try harder! They're up there right now! Don't you believe me?"

As she just finished asking this, the train had come around the room again but abruptly stopped. There was no village or other reason for that to happen. Matt spoke up in a kind voice and said to Elsie, "I believe you, honey!"

That prompted a chorus of the others saying the same and as they did, the train started to move again. A loud cheer erupted from the group and Jesse exclaimed, "Did you see that? We made it happen! The angels are listening to us!"

This time however, when the train again went into the back room, it didn't come out.

Horace asked Elsie, "What's happening now, honey? Are the angels still here?"

"Yes, but I think they are leaving now!"

But suddenly she broke out in a smile and exclaimed, "They just told me that they will be back again next Christmas Eve!"

With that everyone in the room again wore big smiles. Horace walked over by Julie and said, "It looks like we're getting a little bit of a real Christmas here tonight. I don't know a time that I felt more in the mood!"

"Yes, it sure brought the old place back to life, didn't it?"

A memory crept back into her mind, and she started walking around the room as if she were looking for something. Returning with a smile on her face, she said to Horace softly, "How would you like to help me lift our little Christmas celebration up another notch?"

He answered with some excitement of his own, like a child being let in on a great hiding place in a game of hide and seek, "Why certainly! What can I do?"

They huddled together there for a moment sharing the scheme. After that they separated, with Julie going to the back room and Horace moving near the glass counter where he had found the toy soldiers earlier. All of a sudden the room went dark, and there were several groans. Charles instinctively called out, "Everyone just keep still for a few minutes! The power went out again as it did earlier. It'll just take a minute or two for me to get back to the maintenance shop and turn the generator on!"

Just as the words passed from his lips, however, red and green lights came on all along the route of the elevated toy train tracks. The earlier groans were replaced with repeated oohs and ahs.

The show continued with all the glass counters being lit up with white lights and that made many of the items inside them shimmer. The entry doorway followed. Despite the busted glass it became an arch of lights with all the familiar Christmas colors.

Finally, on the opposite side of the room, up on the raised platform that held the antique furniture, there was a table. On top of it was a little Christmas tree that was also illuminated, and this showed that the source was strings of miniature lights and ornaments. Under the tree was a manger scene with all the expected characters. Another chorus of pleasant sighs filled the room.

Julie had gone up to her little train platform and was looking down at the room with all of its surprised occupants. It was from there that she had turned on the various Christmas lights just after Horace had shut out the main ones that had, until then, lit the shop.

Julie chose this moment to speak up tenderly with, "When I was a little girl, my father had a Christmas Eve ritual here that the two of us would share late in the night, at the dawn of Christmas. I would have been sleeping on a cot in the back room and he would awaken me by saying, 'Wake up honey, it's time! The train just came in for a delivery while you slept.'

"With the room lit up just the way it is now, he would lead me to the front by the furniture display. After removing a section of the rope that normally held folks back, he would help me step up on the platform and then we each took a seat in the old chairs by the table. On top of it there would be two special ivory colored china cups, decorated with red and green bells. Each was filled with hot chocolate. Mine was at just the right temperature so I wouldn't burn myself. Then dad would raise his cup with the steam swirling upward and exclaim, "Now let us share a toast my dear, to another Christmas that we have brought back the perfect tree!"

"And I would say in reply with a smile, while raising my own cup, 'To the perfect tree and my perfect train, the "Anabelle Lee!'

That's what I had named her. This was a truly special night for me. It was in fact the only night of the year that anyone was allowed to sit on the furniture in dad's display."

Julie added after a moment of quiet, "I hope that none of you will mind that I take this opportunity to say a little prayer."

No one spoke, so she said softly, "Lord, I know you are here with us, and you have already given so much today. Please don't think I'm ungrateful as I make one last wish?"

The group all stood and wondered what she was wishing for, except for Stash who thought that he understood. When she came back to the front by him he whispered, "Honey, I'm praying for your wish too!"

With that they hugged and basked in the glow with little Johnny. The room of people slowly gained back their voices, and it now sounded like they were all loving relatives sharing the holy day.

Suddenly the calm was broken with the loud closing thud of the back door to the maintenance area. Just after that a young black woman rushed into the shop. Charles looked at her with surprise and exclaimed, "Gala, honey, what are you doing here?"

Elsie joined in with, "Mommy, mommy!" And she ran across the room to greet her.

As they hugged, Gala replied, "Oh, Charles, I'm so glad I got here before you left! The trains aren't running because of one that derailed tonight in Blue Island! I was so worried about you getting stranded with Elsie and the weather was so terrible!"

Waiting for her to finish, Charles asked intently, "But, honey, how did you get here?"

"Mother drove me down. She's waiting outside in her car."

"You two are talking again?"

"Yes, Charles, I called her like you said!"

Charles gave her a big hug, and Elsie snuggled up next to them both. After that, Charles saw Jim smiling at them, and he brought Gala over to meet him. He said, "Honey, this is Mr. Smithers. Mr. Smithers, this is my wife, Gala."

After making their goodbyes to everyone, they continued with pleasant conversation while heading toward the exit door. Elsie had grabbed Jim's hand again, and the two walked together. Jim stopped by Julie, Stash, and Ben who were grouped together and said, "Julie, I doubt that you remember me, but many years ago I played cards with your dad and Ben and Vito when he still had the barbershop across the street. We played right in here at a little fold-out table. You name it, and we played it then, Hearts, Gin Rummy, Euker, Poker, and Pinochle. Those were the best of times! Unfortunately, I got switched to the late shift, and I couldn't join them anymore."

After a brief lull, Jim added, "Do you know, Julie, I can still remember your running that train around the shop?

"Your dad would call out to you, 'Where are we headed to today, conductor?'

"I remember you always having an answer. You were certainly going to a lot of places. It was fun to listen to you describing them. I have to tell you when that train started going around tonight by itself, it gave me goosebumps. That was the darndest thing! And that little ritual that you shared with us, that was something real special too!"

Julie took his hand in hers and replied, "I do remember you now, Jim. Thanks for bringing it all back to me!"

Jim then offered Ben his hand while saying, "Merry Christmas, old friend! I know that Frank's disappearance must have been quite a trial for you!"

"That's true, Jim. Things were a bit worrisome there for awhile. All's well that ends well though. I'm in high spirits now!"

Jim nodded and smiled and turned back to Julie, saying, "I was so glad to hear that your dad's alright! Don't you worry about the broken door and glass! As soon as I get outside I'll call my guy on the third shift and tell him to get it all fixed up!"

Julie and Stash both thanked him again.

Jim started yet again to leave with Elsie, but in his common manner of satisfying a curiosity, he turned back and asked Julie, 'Anabelle Lee?' You said that's the name of your train. I know I've heard that somewhere before. I could have sworn it was in a song though!"

"Knowing now, that you had spent time with Ben years ago, I'm not surprised. He used to sing a little ditty about a train named the 'Annabelle Lee' and that's where I got it from."

Ben smiled large as he took all this in. Hearing it Jim exclaimed, "I knew it! I knew it was a song!"

Jim's excitement attracted the others. All but Gala and Charles formed a circle around Ben. Charles was inclined to join them too and pulled on Gala's arm, but she said, "Honey, we can't. I left mom parked by the maintenance unloading door in the back where you have me pick you up sometimes. It's been a little while, and she's probably getting concerned with what happened to me! We have to go and get her!"

"You know, you're right and I have some really good news to tell on our way to get her!"

She interrupted him with, "Don't forget Elsie!"

Jim must have heard her name called out and turned around while still holding the child in his arms. Charles said to him, "We'll be right back, ok?"

Jim replied, "She'll be fine!"

As they passed into the back room Gala shrieked ecstatically, "A promotion!"

Charles tried unsuccessfully to quiet her down. Jim and the others couldn't help but smile. Just seconds passed and she shrieked out again with, "A bonus too!"

And the group all smiled even larger. Horace couldn't contain himself as he exclaimed, "What a night! What a wonderful night!"

Jim looked back at Ben and asked, "Would you do me a great favor and share a verse or two of that song? This isn't the first time that tune has haunted me. It has come and gone several times through the years, but I just couldn't put it together. There was something about pickin' and lookin', lookin' and pickin'."

Ben answered while moving into a thoughtful stance, "Well it's been a long long time. I sang it around here for Julie nearly as often as I did for my sweet wife and my boy. After I lost them, though, I didn't have the heart to do it anymore!"

Jim quickly added, "Oh no, I'm sorry for asking! I wouldn't want you to bring back painful memories!"

"No, please Jim, don't fret about it! I'm beyond that now. I believe I'm not long from being with them again anyway. Before telling you the song, though, it's only proper in holding to a tradition started by my father to explain the situation that made the song come to be."

Jesse moved in close by him as he started with, "It all started with my father's father, my Grandpa Ben Simms, who I was named after. Grandpa, when just a young boy, was a slave on a tobacco farm down south. With the coming of the war all the men of the plantation owner's family went to fight. Not one of them came back.

"Grandpa was eager to break away and see the world around him. He was just 15 years old and a million dreams were waiting for this opportunity. Fate, though, would step in front of him in the form of a sweet and beautiful young girl named Lily. She certainly appeared to be enchanted with him as he was with her. He couldn't, however, convince the girl to leave with him.

"Her grandpa and grandma were amongst five older folks who couldn't deal with such a big change in their lives. Tobacco farming was all that they knew, and Lily was determined to stay with them. She had been separated from her parents when just a baby and was determined not to have it happen again with her remaining kin.

"So while several other young boys and girls left to seek new lives, Grandpa hung on, hoping to find an answer that would work for him and Lily. One would not come though to free him from the burden of his youth. He finally gave in and offered to help the owner's wife run the farm. She was by that time quite perplexed with what to do. In time she became indebted to Grandpa for encouraging some others who had left nearby farms to stay on there too. They all remained even after the missus left.

"She had told grandpa that he could keep anything he could make off the land as long as he took care of the place while she tried to sell it. He did this and managed with small crops of tobacco to get by. It became the only place that grandfather would experience. In time he and Lily would raise their children there, the oldest of which was my father, Thomas.

"Thomas grew into an intelligent young man, and they raised more and more tobacco thanks mostly to his ingenuity. He learned most everything there was to learn about tobacco by working a job for a merchant besides his normal duties on the farm. He knew by checking which tobacco sold for the best price what he in turn should be growing.

"Dad took his pay in young plants, and the seller was quite amazed at how successful he was with growing and drying them. In time, my father became a sought-after supplier and seller in his own right.

"Some people were jealous of his success and tried, on different occasions, to sabotage the crops or steal them. He could only see things getting worse so he planned to move the whole of his family up north to Chicago. There he would start a tobacco-selling business of his own. The result of his trials was the shop he opened across the street. He raised his family here and I, as his oldest boy, would in time be trained to follow in his footsteps. Unfortunately, Grandpa died before the family moved.

"The song that you referred to was made up by my grandfather. The plantation they worked on was split in two by the coming of the railroad. Grandpa and all the others would stop and stare each time the trains would go by. By some agreement with the landowner's wife a water station was built there. It became a regular scheme for the steam locomotives to stop. Dad said that they could mark different times of the day by the trains that passed through.

"It should be noted now that despite some exposure to Christian teaching, my grandfather had not been inspired. He was just a young boy when a preacher named Jeremiah Jones would come and threaten whites and blacks alike with hell and brimstone. Grandpa was more interested though in getting a break after service to go fishin' in a creek nearby.

"The word was that Jeremiah went to war with all the rest. When it was over, there was talk again that he was returning to do his preaching. There was a great deal of high expectations for the return of the man with the thundering voice. One day though he was invited by the missus, and it soon became clear he was but a shell of the human dynamo that he had been.

"Apparently he had stood up in battle to coax his fellow soldiers to advance against a fence line of firing rifles when he himself was shot in the throat. It was doubted that he would survive at all, but the fellow managed to fare in that respect better than so many others.

"In any case, try as he might, and the man was quite determined, he couldn't exhort the words of the Lord in much above a whisper. It was, in fact, difficult for someone standing but a few feet away to understand him at all. Still, in respect for what he was attempting and for the reputation of his past, people would try. This did little though to bring Grandpa over to Christian ways.

"This was a case of God letting one door close and opening another. A whirlwind of sorts came in with the new train line. His name was Milton Franks, an engineer that was on the regular schedule of trains coming their way.

"Milton who's nickname was 'Millrott,' one I must say that was assigned to him unjustly, had a mission in life not unlike Jeremiah. His method and message though stood in great contrast. Milton was inspired to use each and every stop of his train to bellow out the Lord's teachings and considered himself a success if even one person could be enticed to listen. Water stops became one of his most valued opportunities. This brought him right smack into a willing audience on the plantation that my grandfather worked on.

"Grandpa would say that Milton's approach was attractive to him because he was quite the showman. He would preach from the train even as it slowed down for the stop. When the water feeding was over he could still be heard as the train faded into the distance.

"The most appealing aspect of the preaching to Grandpa was that Milton inspired hope by preaching love. Not once did he dwell on the fires of hell in a way that suggested it was a foregone conclusion for most folk, as Jeremiah had. No, Milton was more apt to make folks consider the wonder of God and the heaven where he resides. Grandpa couldn't believe anything less. He felt if God couldn't offer something better than the toil of this life, then he wasn't much of a God at all.

"One beautiful late spring morning, when my dad was an adult and Grandpa was getting on in age, the latter was working near the water tank when Milton brought a new train in. It looked fancy compared to the others they had experienced, with a shiny new black coat of paint. He also saw something painted in white letters on the side of the engineer's compartment. As Milton was engaged in his usual bout of exuberance, Grandpa called to my dad to tell him what the words meant, because he had never learned to read himself.

"Dad came up and was quite surprised. He told him that it read as follows, 'If you want to get a little closer to heaven, take a ride on the "Annabelle Lee!'

"My dad said that Grandpa was quite taken in by this, like it was some kind of a sign. He said back to him then with earnest, 'I lost my notions to leave this place after I settled with your momma. It wasn't actually that hard to stay. Unlike many in other places that I've heard tell of, I worked and was fed without fear of a master's whip in my younger years. When he and his boys were taken in battle, I was left with the means to provide for me and mine.

'Someday though, the Lord will take me. I expect sooner rather than later. I imagine that this would be a fine way to go and meet him, riding in a vessel as great as this is! I would smile and wave my hat as it passed through the pearly gates. I could picture myself now inside the 'Annabelle Lee,' getting closer to heaven and God's open arms!

"Dad said that this was a side of grandpa that he had never experienced. He was normally quiet and kept to himself. He remembered how his dad proceeded to spend long evenings for several days making up and memorizing the words and tune to a song. When finally he thought that grandpa was finished, dad wrote the words down that he had sung.

"They went like this:

I've spent my life pickin' and lookin'
Waitin' for a sign
Walkin' that troublesome line
Passin' some bits of time

I'm comin' Lord
You can surely tell
I've walked right past that pit of Hell
Would you look at me
In the Annabelle Lee?

I've spent my life lookin' and pickin'
What will I do when you call?
Which way do I go y'all?
Hope I'm not in for a fall

*I'm comin' Lord
You can surely tell
I've walked right past that pit of Hell
Would you look at me
In the Annabelle Lee?*

*All the time I knew
When my livin' time was finally through
There'd be nuthin' left that I could do
While you were pickin' and lookin'*

*I'm comin' Lord
You can surely tell
I've walked right past that pit of Hell
Would you look at me
In the Annabelle Lee?*

*Should you look with favor
On my life, most filled with labor
I am sure only then to savor
Your pickin' and lookin'*

*I'm comin' Lord
Right up above
My soul is filled with nothin' but love
As you ride into heaven with me
In the Annabelle Lee*

Jim couldn't help but applaud when the finish was certain and, the others joined in as he exclaimed, "That was so much more than I had hoped for! Well done! Very well done!"

By this time, Charles and Gala had returned. Jim and Elsie joined them where they were patiently waiting by the door. They were just in time to hear Jesse ask Ben, "Mr. Simms, did you ever find out more about the guy named Weatherbee and the book that he carried?"

To respond, Ben first had to fill everyone in on the background information he had shared with Jesse earlier. After that he commented, "As a matter of fact, to answer your question, Jesse, it was many years later that I got to see that man again. It was, I recall, in the summer of 1956. I remember because Frank had shut his shop down for remodeling and was bringing in some new items to display. He had just reopened it on the day that this fellow Weatherbee showed up in my place. He introduced himself as Lawrence Weatherbee and told me that he knew my father and was asking after him."

Hearing this name, Julie suddenly became more alert and listened intently to the details of all that was being said. Ben continued with, "I had to tell him that dad was gone already for quite some time by then. He was, as my dad had told me, a very personable fellow, and I realized something that had never before been stated. He was a colored man and that was probably why dad had felt so comfortable asking his advice.

"Another thing that stood out was his obvious interest in Frank's store. He kept looking over at it through my window. I received one new bit of information then that my dad had never confided. Dad had told Lawrence how his true goal as a young man was to travel. Like his father though, looking after others became his lot in life. Also like Grandpa he was enthralled by what train travel could offer. He wasn't thinking past his life though as Grandpa had. He wanted to ride trains all over the country as Milton Frank did.

"In fact the highlight of his life was one time when Milton took him with on an overnight run going north through the mountains. Milton taught him all about running an engine, and dad helped him in every way that he could. Dad was only twelve years old and that experience imprinted on him like none other had. Fate dealt him a world of tobacco, but even when it came time to move everyone up north, dad picked Chicago because it was known as the railroad hub of the country.

"All of this shined a new light on an experience that I had shared with dad back in 1949. There was a large railroad show in Chicago that year and daddy took me with him. It had been held over from the year before, and dad wanted badly to see it. I remember being very busy with the shop, and because I would be taking over responsibility for running the business, I didn't want to leave.

"Dad, though, insisted. He said that I would have my whole life to work, but the railroad show was a once in a lifetime event. When we were there and took a break to eat, a fellow shared the table with us. He worked for a company that built trains, and the conversation held dad's full attention.

"When the man told him how the new modern diesel engine trains were the way of the future and that steam engines were on their way out, I could see dad getting a little tear in his eye. I thought after discovering dad's passion that he was probably reminiscing that day about his boyhood experience with Milton. Daddy died later that year, and I wish we had more experiences with just the two of us.

"After our conversation about dad had ended, Lawrence asked what time the antique shop opened. I explained how Frank had been changing the place and that he picked a good day to come by because the shop was just reopening. He seemed to be relieved by hearing this.

"I have to tell you, though, that another thing that caught my attention in that visit was that Lawrence was carrying a book like the one that my daddy had described. It seemed to me to be too much of a coincidence to be the same one, but I couldn't help myself and started to ask him about it.

"Well darned be all if that wasn't just when Frank appeared across the street opening his door. Lawrence spotted him and was up in a flash and apologizing to me for a quick goodbye. Before I could say three words he was halfway over there dodging through the traffic. I never saw a man his age so determined. He was oblivious to the cars honking their horns and weaving around him.

"To my disappointment several customers came into my place right at that time, or I would have followed him over there. By the time I finished, no one was in the shop but

Frank. I asked him about the man and what kind of business he was seeking, but Frank said he just looked around for a few minutes and left.

"I was so sad. I felt that I had lost my big chance to find out about something that had been a real curiosity to my dad. I'm sorry to say that I never saw or heard from the fellow again. He looked quite old and I imagine he didn't live long after that."

Julie couldn't hold back herself any longer and spoke up excitedly with, "I think I might have the answer to your riddle in the shop somewhere!"

This got the attention of all that were listening. They watched as she started inspecting all the books around the room. She looked at those on the table and a few that were still on the floor and finally she returned to the bookcases. She looked earnestly through the rows checking each book by its title. Frustration was taking over though as she obviously was not finding the object of her search.

Finally she cried out, "Oh Lord, I hope it wasn't sold. I had taped a note in it that it was not for sale. I should have packed it away somewhere safe! Oh my, it was so special!"

All of a sudden the group started helping her by bringing books that had fallen but were pushed into places out of view. It seemed that this too was futile, when Elsie walked up to her with one and said, "How about this?"

Julie was ready to discount it, when suddenly she shrieked, "Wait, that's it!"

She opened it carefully to the first pages and then looked over to Ben lovingly and said, "Ben, you have to see this! I knew I remembered that name!"

Ben did as she said while all the others circled them. She told him to read the foreword to the book. As he did he saw first the book's title, The Legend of *Non-A-Me,* and then as he started reading the foreword, he discovered that it was written by none other than a Lawrence Weatherbee! From that passage he quickly realized that the book was in fact very special to Lawrence, and now he had some grasp of why.

He held it tenderly, thinking that he had finally received the answer his father and then he himself had longed for. It was obviously not a ledger or compilation of business notes as had been expected. It was a storybook! Inside his heart this made him determined to discover why this man, after obviously treasuring it for so many years, decided to place it in Frank's shop.

Ben asked Julie oh-so tenderly, "Honey, can I take this for a while to read? I'll be very careful with it. I'll have to use a magnifier because I don't see so good anymore. But I just got to read it!"

Jesse jumped in with, "I'll read it to you, Mr. Simms!"

"That would be real nice Jesse, if that's ok with Julie!"

"Ben, I can only surmise from all that has happened here tonight, that you were meant to have it."

He was taken aback by her response and hugged her as tears flushed from his old eyes. Each of those standing by glanced at the old book and found it quite special that the things the man had been wondering about were answered by it.

It had been a long day and night though and they all were considering how they would be going home. Jim and little Elsie moved first to join Gala and Charles. They all exited carefully over the ice and reached the car. Jim was in the midst of giving his goodbyes when Gala's mom got out and walked toward them. She exclaimed, "Well, I see that everyone is ok. I tried to tell her, Charles, that you were very capable of taking care of my little sweetheart!"

She reached out her arms, and Elsie ran to her for a big hug. Charles, seeing Jim standing and smiling at this said, "Mr. Smithers, this is my mother-in-law, Elsie."

"Well, how nice!"

She approached him, and he shook her hand while adding, "I have now had the pleasure of meeting two beautiful Elsies today!"

"Well, you are so kind, Mr. Smithers!"

"Please, call me, Jim!"

Gala and Charles broke out in smiles, and Gala couldn't miss the opportunity to ask, "Jim, could we drop you off somewhere?"

"Oh, I couldn't bother you for that!"

But the older Elsie quickly interjected, "Why, it's no bother at all!"

After which she looked at Gala and Charles while saying, "You kids sit in the back, would you? Jim here is a big man. He needs to sit up front to get enough leg room!"

Jim replied, "That's very considerate of you, Elsie!"

With that they were all smiling as the car took off into the night. Gala soon broke the silence though with, "So what should we talk about on this most special Christmas Eve?"

Before anyone else could respond, little Elsie piped in with, "Mr. Smithers, could you tell them about the Annabelle Lee?"

"You mean the part about the song?"

"No, I mean the whole story, starting with the manger scene. And don't forget the train with the angels and the little girl and her daddy drinking hot chocolate by the Christmas tree and then the part with the song."

They all laughed, and Gala piped in with,

"Now, honey, you can't expect Mr. Smithers to tell us all of that! Though I must say that you've got me wondering now what I missed here tonight!"

Jim spoke up with, "That's quite alright! I really don't mind. All I need to do first is make that phone call about getting the door fixed that I promised Julie. How about this Elsie, if I forget anything in the story, you just tell me, ok?"

She replied happily, "I will! And they all broke out in smiles again.

* * *

Many miles away in Indiana, while Vela was showing Frank to his room, they passed a door with a card taped to it. Frank couldn't help but read the words, "Dorothy Fleming."

He stopped and just stood there, stunned. Finally he asked, "Vela, what is this place, some kind of hospital?"

She looked over at him and answered, "It's a hospice. That's where people come to die with some dignity."

"And is she dying too?"

There was a pause and finally she answered, "I'm sorry to do this to you, Mr. Fleming! We had no idea that you would be coming tonight!"

He asked again, "Is she dying?"

"I don't think she'll make it to the morning."

Frank looked back at her in disbelief. Seeing his reaction, she added, "She was doing so well. That's why Julie thought she could leave and it would be ok. It just came on suddenly, poor thing!"

Frank just stood there thinking of how he had wondered what happened to her. When he read through Julie's letters, and she didn't mention her mom, he assumed that she had already died.

Memories of his time with her flooded his mind. When she left he justified his bad feelings with concern for Julie. The fact was that he hated Dorothy because she left him. Until that time she had been the center of his universe. In his heart he wallowed in a state of self pity. When Julie left to be with her it was like another rejection. It brought back all of the bad feelings that he had felt for Dorothy.

In time all of the ill will became like millstones fastened to his heart with chains. Secretly he had hoped to be rid of them, but he maintained the appearance of the sad situation through his stubbornness. Suddenly now the opportunity to cut the chains loose was just beyond this door. If only he could find the courage, if only she could hear him.

He lifted his shaking hand to the door handle. It cracked open, and he could see the girl of his youth, now old and gray, lying there still in a lace white nightgown. He approached the bed and looked down at her as old memory glimpses continued to fill his mind. He knelt down and put his hand on hers. For the second time that night he started to cry.

With his head bowed down he heard a low voice, "Julie, Julie, honey, is that you?"

For a moment there was silence, and then Frank responded softly with, "No, Dorothy, it's Frank."

Her body moved suddenly as she did all she could to see him. When their eyes finally met she exclaimed with the little energy that she could muster, "Oh Frank is that really you?"

After focusing briefly, she added, "Oh it is you! Thank you so much for coming to me, Frank. It's all that I wished for, prayed for!"

She stopped speaking to catch her breath. He felt her hand turn to cup his and she added, "Thank you, Frank, for giving me the chance to say I'm sorry. Please forgive me! I treated you so badly. You were always so good to me."

As another moment passed, Frank fought to form the right words. He got these few out with a stutter, "I forgive you Dorothy, but I fear that I am the one who needs forgiveness."

To this she replied with all the enthusiasm her body could manage, "Forgive you? Oh Frank, you did nothing wrong! Now you've given me this precious moment that I longed for. That is everything to me! There is nothing to forgive."

The night went forward as Frank continued to hold her hand. In the twilight of Christmas, another soul passed over to a finer place. But before leaving, Julie's prayer had been answered.

The End

CPSIA information can be obtained at www.ICGtesting.com
Printed in the USA
LVOW07s0024051213

363910LV00001B/5/P

9 781457 523588